Sierra

A Modern Psychological Thriller

Lee Dawna

LeeDawna Books, Inc.

First edition

Cover design by Premade Ebook Cover Shop

https://www.premadeebookcovershop.com

ISBN 978-1-949192-26-1 (paperback)

ISBN 978-1-949192-25-4 (ebook)

Published by LeeDawna Books, Inc.

https://leedawnabooks.com

leedawnabooks@gmail.com

P.O. Box 205, MacArthur WV 25873

~

For Bobbi. Wait for it...

~

~ 1 ~

June 25, 2012

Hey. What's up?

Yeah, you. The person snooping through my personal belongings and reading my diary.

Still here? Of course you are. Nosy people always keep reading. At least the houseful of sisters I'm trapped with do. They like to stick their noses where they don't belong, so I might as well make everyone's meddling worth it. For me. Because I promise you, by the time you get to the end, you're going to wish you never eavesdropped on my personal thoughts.

I'm walking a dark road...

B.

I close the diary and turn the black fabric book over in my hand. Eleven years have passed since 2012 and it sounds like that was a year as memorable for whoever this B person is as it was for me. I was seventeen back then. That September, Mom moved us out of the trailer we'd lived in my whole life and into this dump of a house. She played it up like this move was prestigious, declaring this big house to be the kind of place people drive by and wish they owned. I agreed with her then the same way I agree now. This house *was* a mark of affluence, way back in the Victorian era when these elaborate homes with their Mansford roofs were in vogue.

If the intricately detailed eaves and decorative brackets weren't crumbling and people with enough money to restore the grandiose home to its original condition owned the place, it would truly be a sight to behold. Mom and I are not those people. Crusty ol' Rusty the landlord isn't either. If he even had the money to take on a renovation project like this, he wouldn't. All Crusty cares about is draining every cent he can out of destitute old drunks like my mom. She's the kind of alcoholic who always puts the bottle first, and it was her dedication to drinking that drove me to run away only a few weeks after she moved us in here. Ironically, her unwavering devotion to alcohol is the very thing that has me back in this hellhole again.

I tuck the diary under my arm and look around. At seventeen, I wasn't curious as to what mysteries a crumbling old house like this could hold. I explored very little. My concern at the time was being forced to move across town, away from my boyfriend. Conner had lived in a trailer fifty feet away from mine since elementary school, the two of us having the convenience of being neighbors in the cramped court where the poorest residents of Poca congregated. When Mom moved us out of there, all I wanted was to go back. The rusted condition of the trailer we'd been living in didn't matter to me. This house was no better, and in many ways, it was worse. One major difference being the absence of my teenage lover.

Outside of my angst, what I remember from my few weeks in this house is the crumbling ceilings and stained floors. This oversized spare bedroom on the second floor was the worst room in the house back in 2012 and it still holds that title today. The ceiling is now caved in above the tall window that's probably been here since the 1800s when this monstrosity was built. The landlord's solution to the hole in the ceiling is a bright blue tarp that stretches over half of the pitched roof and down to the center of the flat Mansford-style part of the roof. That might stop the rain from ruining more of the house, but it doesn't fix the damage already done. Now that I'm twenty-eight instead of a seventeen-year-old lovesick kid, I don't intend to let Crusty get away with being a slumlord any longer.

While I'm forcing Crusty into action, I'll figure out who this B is too. If they're still in Poca, they'd probably like to have their diary back. It's remarkable the book even survived living inside the tiny nook of this room for the last eleven years. The little padded seat built into the corner hadn't escaped my notice, but I didn't realize the seat lifted up until today. I only discovered it because I was trying to pull back the rotting fabric so I could see how badly the wood beneath is damaged.

I pick my way across the spongy floor and leave the room, closing the door behind me, a sneeze ripping out as I tug the dusty piece of thick clear plastic back across the door. This piece of plastic is *Mom's* solution to fixing the water leak. Block the room off and don't go inside. Out of sight, and it doesn't exist for her. An attitude that makes her a perfect tenant for Crusty.

"Mom?" I snake through the creaking narrow halls and tread carefully down the steep steps, groaning when my shoulder bangs into the thick wood encasing the doorway to what Mom calls her sitting room. I call it the mold room. The plaster ceiling is cracked like it was always meant to resemble a spider web and in the corner with the actual spider webs, there's a spotty black film showing where the water leaks down to this floor from the one above it. I'm not sure how long it takes a leaky roof to ruin two floors of ceilings, but the mold has gotten worse since I was a teenager and there's no doubt in my mind that behind the plaster is a whole mess of rotten wood.

"Mom, let me help you." I plop the diary on the scratchy wool couch that came with the *furnished* house. Instead of admitting she moved us into squalor, Mom bounced around the house like a yo-yo, declaring her joy over having such a home. An excitement born from the landlord being the owner of the bar down the street. Try as she might have, I wasn't fooled by her proclamations of this place being our fresh start. Her joy was solely a product of this home's location. Because other than mold, the only thing that changed between the trailer court and here was the amount of exercise her legs got. Walking two blocks instead of four miles was better whether she was sober or drunk.

Not that her bar walks were ever a full eight mile round-trip. Most nights, she didn't make it home. Anytime she didn't shack up with a man, I could find her somewhere between the trailer and the bar, passed out in a ditch or on someone's front lawn.

"I don't need your help," Mom barks out, her cane wobbling under her unsteady grip. The rubber soles of the four-pronged base catch on the scuffed old hardwood, spots of long-forgotten stains everywhere the eye can see.

I grip her arm and ease her toward the stiff chair sitting in front of a television that still has an antenna on it. The thing doesn't work anymore but she has a portable DVD player sitting on top of it with a scratched-up copy of *Pretty Woman* constantly playing on repeat. "You need more help than I can give you, but I'm all you've got, so stop fighting me and just sit down."

She yanks her arm, trying to shake me loose, but the alcohol has drained her of the strength she used to have when I was a kid. Now, she's feeble at best. No longer capable of backhanding me. I lead her to the seat and settle her on the hard cushion. After Mom's last episode, when Aunt Diana found her passed out on the floor and bleeding from the mouth, I had to face the reality that Mom can't live alone anymore. "Your health is in a nosedive, Mom. That's why Aunt Di called me. She can't stay here with you and she can't keep making the hour commute to check on you every day."

Mom launches a wad of spit at my face, the white foam missing its mark and landing on her own arm instead. Her beady mud-brown eyes harden. "She's not your aunt. She's nothing to you. Like I'm nothing to you. I don't even know who you are."

Guilt itches my insides. No matter what she did to me when I was a kid, beatings she called discipline or letting the random men she shacked up with knock me around, she always had a way of making me feel like everything was my fault. If I'd been prettier, quieter, smarter, or didn't eat so much or ask too many questions, maybe I wouldn't get slapped across the face. In my heart, I knew it wasn't true, but my head always told me it was. Because every single time there was a problem, Mom somehow managed to be the victim. Not me. "If you didn't want me here, you should have stopped drinking when I left."

Her one-syllable laugh carries all of the cruelty I've known from her. "You didn't leave, you ran. Like the coward you are."

She's not entirely wrong. I left because I couldn't handle being here anymore and back then, I had Conner. He gave me an escape from her. Kept me sane. When Mom was passed out in public, he'd even help me get her home. Conner gave me a slice of life that was all my own. Instead of me sitting beside Mom's bed making sure she didn't choke on her own vomit, Conner would pull me away, tell me that her choices were wholly her own and that I had to let her face the consequences. He's the only person who ever knew my pain, and he hated how she treated me as much as I did.

Sometimes Conner and I talked about running off together after graduation, leaving *everyone* in Poca to deal with their own choices while the two of us saw the world together. I guess you could say I pulled the trigger on that dream a little early, fleeing Poca when mine and Conner's last year of high school was just beginning. It broke my heart to leave him but I was never Conner's one and only the way he was my everything. I was a convenience for him, and I never felt the truth of that more than when Mom moved us into the heart of a mold infestation. I barely saw him those last few weeks in Poca so I didn't even tell him I was leaving. I just packed up and walked out of town, making it as far as Texas before I ended my cross-country trip. The only person I ever bothered to check in with over the years was Aunt Di, and I've only spoken to her three whole times since leaving Poca.

I grab a tissue and wipe the spit off Mom's arm. There's a leatheriness to the translucent skin stretched over her bones, the look aging her beyond her years. She's always been skinny and prematurely wrinkled, compliments of a life lived at the bottom of a liquor bottle, but the past eleven years have not been kind to her. She's skeletal, pale, and what's left of her once brown hair is more silver than not. "I did cower from you, Mom. Yet it was still my name you would scream out in the middle of the night when one of your lowlife boyfriends was beating you up. *Sierra! Sierra!*" I mock the way she used to yell for me when I was only a kid. "I'm not five years old anymore, and I don't need you to scream my name for me to know that you need help. I can see that just by looking at you. So don't get up again unless it's for food or the bathroom because I already scoured every inch of this place, even the condemned room above this one. All your hidden booze is gone."

She points a bony finger up at me. "You never came when I called. Only the devil did."

I blow out a frustrated breath. Her watery, bloodshot eyes meet mine. "Get away from me, *Sierra*. Having a daughter like you is a worse curse than what I got out of that bottle. That's why I told Diana not to bother calling the likes of you here. If I want to die, I'll do it on my own. I don't need you here getting me to my grave any quicker."

I blink, fighting the tears that want to surface. I refuse to let them. I won't cry in front of her anymore. I'm not going to give her the satisfaction of knowing how deeply her words hurt. "It's the liquor that's hastening you to death's door. Between diabetes and the medication you're on, you know you're not supposed to be drinking. Why can't you just stop?"

Her nose crinkles, chapped lips turning up in disgust. "I'll make a deal with you. I'll stop drinking on the day *you* die."

I turn away from her and pick up the diary. "We're living forever then because I'll only die on the day you win a mother-of-the-year award."

~2~

I knew coming back to Poca would be a tribulation all its own. A lesson in misery. One bolstered by the misfortune of having an alcoholic for a mother and made worse by having a mother who hates the very sight of me. Her words and actions can't be passed off as only the alcohol talking because liquor isn't what makes Mom despise me. I'm entirely sure that her drinking is a result of some type of motherly guilt she feels over being a woman who hates her child. Aunt Diana once told me that she never saw my mom drink a drop until after I was born, and I've seen news reports about postpartum and the awful things mothers do to their children when they're suffering from what has to be the deepest kind of depression. Instead of harming me, Mom self-medicated her way straight to alcoholism.

I guess that will happen when you're alone, suffering, and financially struggling to raise a child whose father you couldn't pick out of a lineup if all of the men you slept with came forward to claim the prize of a squalling mouth to feed. Aunt Di also told me that Mom was *loose* when they were growing up, convinced a man was going to love what was between her legs enough to whisk her away from the poverty surrounding them. The only thing she got out of that way of thinking was me. Every time I asked Mom about my dad, she said I'd find out who he is when I die because we were all going to be reunited in Hell. A proclamation that made nightmares appear before I was even nine years old. I'd wake up covered in sweat and occasionally find blood on my hands. In my sleep, I'd claw at my face and arms, trying to put out the flames my dreams were full of.

Those dreams made me chew my nails practically off. People in school would make fun of me for biting them down to the quick but I never could break the habit because if I let them grow, I'd end up with claw marks that the kids would also make fun of. I guess maybe that's what inspired me to become the self-taught nail technician I am today. After I got out of Poca and settled in Dallas, I started healing my nails, and learning all the ways to paint and lengthen them.

Six months later, for once in my life, I had pretty nails. So much so that random women would stop me to ask where I got them done. That led me to going into the homes of some of those women to do their nails, and that led to more clients. While most salons wouldn't let me work under their brand because I had no formal training, Becky was friends with one of my clients so she let me rent a booth. I had no set schedule because I still did house calls and Becky only cared that I paid my booth rental every month, so I worked inside the salon as little or as much as I wanted. Having nothing better to do with my time, I worked a lot.

I park my little blue rental car in the last row of spots outside the library. In Dallas, I didn't need a car. My one-room apartment was within walking distance of everything I needed and when I had to go into the fancy neighborhoods my clients lived in, I'd either call for a car or they'd send one for me. Either way, my expenses were nominal. I saved every penny I could, steadily growing my bank account. Not that I was saving for anything in particular. I just wanted to know that I had a nest egg for whatever the future might bring my way, hoping that future would be filled with sunny days and opportunities. Instead, I gave up my booth, my apartment, and paid for a full month's use of a rental car just so I could travel back across the country for an alcoholic who in two full days, has refused to have a single civil conversation with me.

I step out of the car and look around. Poca is a one-traffic-light kind of town. The type of place people live when they despise city life. Being the last stop on the pinwheel of suburbs surrounding the neighboring cities, Poca is as far as you can go before you hit nothing but open country. I doubt I could make any money here even if I did find a salon to rent a booth in, so I hope that by the time I'm feeling the strain in my savings, Mom's immediate health concerns will be taken care of. Then I can spread my wings and fly right back out of here.

A bell rings in the school building behind the library. I would smile, but the memories I have of going to school here are about as bleak as the ones I have of Mom. Clutching the diary, I head for the front of the wood-sided library. Despite how short my trip has been I still already need a break from being in close proximity to Mom. There's no better place to find sanctuary than the library. I hope. I've honestly never been much of a reader but this ominous-sounding diary has me curious and it's as good of a reason as any to get away from Mom for a while. If the date on the first entry is right, I would have still been living in the trailer park. B's family must have lived in the rotting Victorian before Mom moved in.

Poca isn't that big of a town so I should recognize the name of B's family if I can find it in the property records, assuming they owned the house before Crusty got his grimy hands on it. If they were only tenants, I'll have to ask him who they were because right now, I can only remember one girl whose name started with a B and she didn't have any sisters. Billie was an only child, same as me.

I pass the stone benches lining the sidewalk just as the rumble of a lawnmower makes its way around the side of the building. I glance in that direction, my eyes forcing my whole body to freeze as they land on a mop of messy dark hair that I couldn't forget even if I actually tried to. My heart hammers, the lawnmower Conner's on drowning out the sound, but I can still feel the destruction happening under my shirt. I knew there was a chance I'd see him, but unlike the few minutes when I thought I could ask Mom about the diary, I never once thought to ask her about Conner. She never liked him, mainly because she couldn't understand what he saw in me, so mentioning Conner's name in her presence was just asking for trouble. Now I'm the one in trouble. I thought that *if* Conner was still in town, I'd have more time to figure out what I should say to him before casually bumping into him. I don't recall him reading a single book for fun so I drove here without ever expecting our casual encounter to happen at the library.

I lean my head forward, hoping my strawberry-blonde locks will hide my face from him. My cut is short, angled just below my chin, but when Conner knew me, this hair was long and wavy. If he glances up from the lawn he's mowing, he won't know it's me.

I breeze up the steps, nice and fast but not so quick that the movement will draw his attention. After the fight I just had with Mom, the last thing I need is to be forced to look into the face of the boy who stole my virginity right along with my teenage heart. The boards of the library's expansive porch creak under my weight. I cringe, as if the sound can be heard over the lawnmower. *Just breathe, Sierra.* I reach for the door. "Sierra!" His voice rings out, the growl of the lawnmower dying off behind it. I keep my gaze on the door, fingers resting on the knob and my eyes trained on the delicate tin letter K dangling below the oval iron knob.

A few times, I thought about sending Conner a letter. I even picked up the phone and dialed every digit except the last one. Something inside of me always kept me from following through, like I just knew he was better off without me calling him up out of the blue. I even stayed off all social media in an attempt not to see his face. I didn't want to know who he dated after me or how quickly he moved on from us. When I left Poca, I left behind seventeen years.

"Sierra!" Conner shouts my name again. Louder. From closer than before. My mouth goes dry, hand beginning to shake as his footsteps sound on the porch behind me. His body stops behind mine. Too close. I can feel the heat from his skin and smell the musky scent of his sweat mixed with fresh-cut grass and gasoline. "Sierra, what are you doing here?"

I lower my arm to my side and beg my nerves to settle down because pretending I don't hear him is no longer an option. I plaster a fake smile on my face and inhale deeply, slowly releasing the air from my lungs as I turn to face him. Immediately, I regret not running into the library as if I'm not even this Sierra person he's calling out to. Somehow, Conner is even more attractive than he was as a teen. Tall and lined with muscle in a way that only athletes like him are. I never buried all of my old feelings for him and from the way my vision is going dark around the edges, I'd say they're fighting to rise all the way up from my heart to spew out of my mouth.

I shuffle backward a step, right into the library door. The tin K pings against the wood and iron as if it's counting how many seconds I'll stand here staring at Conner's mouth like another thing I'm hankering to do is dive straight into his lips. I lift my eyes, finding his devoid of the youthful glow they once had. That's to be expected, I suppose. I try my smile out again, hoping it looks steadier than I feel. "Hi, Conner. I'm a little jumpy, I guess, but it's good to see you. I just got into town and wondered if you were still around."

He grips my arm, his sunbaked hand yanking me off to the side of the porch. "Don't *hi* me. What in the hell are you doing here?"

I make a show of the diary. "I'm checking out a book."

He knocks the diary out of my hand. It clatters against the wood planks at our feet. "Try again. And without lying this time."

I press a hand to his chest, pushing him out of my personal space while also letting my palm linger on his solid form. I shouldn't touch him like this but he also shouldn't be standing this close to me. "I'm not lying about anything, and I wasn't aware that saying hello to you was a crime or that I needed your permission to visit a library."

He pushes me against the wood siding, trapping my hand between our bodies, his muscles tense and his features hard. "Poca, Sierra. Why are you in Poca?"

I tug my smashed hand free of his chest and try to sidestep but he slams a hand to the wall and boxes me in. I narrow my eyes. "I'm here to spend time with my mom."

He huffs, half coming out as a laugh and the other half pure menace. "You're not here to visit your mom. You couldn't get away from her fast enough and she felt the same damn way about you, so let me tell you what you're doing here. You're leaving, Sierra. Now. Get in that little blue car of yours and get out of Poca. For good this time."

I glance over his shoulder to the parking lot. "How did you know which car is mine?"

"Is there a problem here, Mr. Ferguson?" A uniformed officer tops the stairs and crosses the porch.

Conner steps away from me. "No problem at all. Sierra was just leaving."

"Sierra?" The officer takes off his hat. "Well, look at that. If it ain't the canary that flew off leaving all the cats behind..."

Recognition filters through me. "Luke?"

He chuckles, tapping his chest. "That's Sergeant Putnam, ma'am."

I put more distance between Conner and me by pulling myself away from the siding and taking a step toward Luke. "Followed in your daddy's footsteps, huh? After all that bellyaching about never being like him, now *you're* the Sergeant Putnam who's going to pull me over because you're a bully who likes to throw his weight around?"

Luke's smile fades, his eyes cutting to Conner. "I don't bully people, which is why I had to step up and take this position. There are so few good men in town that we needed someone with integrity to uphold the law."

Conner folds his arms over his chest. "Speaking of stepping, you can head back the way you came. Sierra and I are in the middle of something and we wouldn't want you to ruin your integrity by watching us."

A pain stabs through my gut. Something is going on between the two of them and whatever it is, I don't want to be in the middle of it. And after the reaction Conner just had to seeing me, I don't want to continue doing *anything* with him. I pick the diary up off the porch. "We were finished. Remember? I was just leaving." I keep my eyes off him and put them on Luke, clutching the diary to me for support. "It was good to see you but I want to check something out in the library before they close. Maybe I'll see you around, though. I'm back in town for a while, helping my mom out with some doctors' appointments."

Luke settles his hat back on his head. "I heard she was in bad shape. It's good that you came back from wherever you flew away to." He gives me a wink. "I'll definitely be seeing you, Sierra. You can count on that."

Conner's chest rumbles and I glance between the two men. They used to be friends. Not besties or anything, but not mortal enemies either. Luke struts to the library door and opens it for me. Conner's stone-cold eyes flit to mine, daring me to move. My head buzzes. I underestimated how Conner would react to seeing me again. Before today, I never even saw him angry. The Conner I knew was kind. Gentle. And so full of jokes it was impossible to be in a bad mood around him. Whomever this imposter standing in front of me is, he's glaring at me as if my head belongs on his silver platter.

~ *3* ~

Adrenaline does strange things to a person. I don't remember how I got to this library table or what I said to the pod person posing as Conner before I escaped him to come inside. I don't even remember chatting with Jan at the front desk or filling out the paperwork for a library card. The double-sided application is in front of me, though, and filled out with nicer handwriting than I usually have. Maybe the next time I have to write something by hand I should find Conner again and ask him to manhandle me.

I slide the paper off the table and walk to the counter. Jan smiles, rubbing one hand along her pregnant belly as she takes the application from me. I smile back at her. "When are you due?"

She blows bluntly cut bangs off her forehead. "Three weeks from now, but I swear this boy is coming early. I felt him shift last week and ever since, my right leg has been numb."

I blink. Even when she worked in the office at my high school, she was as cucumber cool as she is now. But a numb leg doesn't seem like something a pregnant woman should be brushing off. "What did your doctor say? Can they get the baby to move?"

She grins. "Honey, this is baby number four. I didn't even call Dr. Siegal about my leg because my last boy settled right in this same spot and did the exact same thing." She focuses back on the computer where she's typing information from my application into her database. "You know how it is. These babies will move when they're good and ready, and after you've had one, you get a feel for when they're going to be good and ready."

I look down at my feet. Part of me feels like I should know how it is, but I don't. I left Poca in a daze, snapshots of buses and hitchhiking all that remain of the fog I was in those first couple of years. I was hungry, cold, and homeless. Sometimes I'd lose track of days at a time. Others, I'd wake up in a strange man's bed. Those were my lowest times, when I felt like my mom but only worse because I was doing what I did while sober. I guess. I blocked it from my memory so I wouldn't have to relive what I did to survive. Unfortunately, the coping mechanism worked a little too well because I still black out and wake up in strange places, like a random bus stop or a man's bed. The only reprieve I have is that now, it only happens when I'm drinking. I guess getting wasted and hooking up with strangers is my version of dating.

"If I ever stop taking birth control maybe I'll figure out what being pregnant is all about." I give her another smile, hoping she doesn't know how lucky I am that one of my early benders didn't result in me getting knocked up. If it would have, I would be *exactly* like Mom, having the baby of a random man whose name I don't even know. If there's anything I want in this world, it's to have my apple falling far, far away from my mom's tree. "You had two kids when I was in high school so that means you've had another since I've been gone?"

She hands me a printout from the noisy old printer beside her. "Yep. All boys. That's why I left my job at the school and took this one. My house is loud enough, I don't need to be around kids at work too." She studies me, eyes dipping to my bare fingers. "What about you? Did you ever finish up high school someplace and settle down with a husband?"

I flash the only thing on my left hand worth seeing, my perfectly manicured nails. I hope she pays attention to them instead of my heated cheeks. I don't know why talking to her about children makes me feel like she knows I've stumbled out of a strange man's bed more times than I care to admit. "No, ma'am. To both questions. I do have a good job though. Well, I did until my aunt called and asked me to come back here to take care of my mom."

Pity sweeps across her face, the corners of her mouth turning down. "You never got a GED or anything? All those years of school just thrown away right in the final stretch?"

I clear my throat. "I went straight to work when I left Poca so it never seemed necessary to get a GED. And I have a good bit of savings to hold me over for a while, so I'm not worried about needing another job just yet. But, um, do you know how I can access property records? Is that something I can do in here?"

She presses a hand back to her stomach and rounds the desk. "Like I told you when you came in, those records will be on the computer over here. What type of job do you have?"

I show her my hand again. "I'm a nail technician at a trendy salon in Dallas. Was, rather."

She glances at my hand and looks away, the sentiment on the turn of her lips a clear one. She doesn't think my job is a valuable one. I doubt anyone in Poca would. Hence the reason I can't make any money here. Not the kind I'm used to. Still, I feel the need to defend myself. "I have...*had* a lot of big-name clients. Some were celebrity status, others just wealthy."

Jan stops by the row of three computers, tapping the seat of the first one for me, still unimpressed with my occupation. "I'm not so sure I wouldn't have been better choosing your path. Stay single, only have responsibility to myself." She rubs her stomach. "This baby here is what you call a surprise. I didn't even think I was young enough to get pregnant again, and now I've told LeRoy that he better plan on spending the rest of his nights on the couch because if the good Lord decides to bless me with another squawking child, I'll probably go to prison for killing that good ol' husband of mine."

~

I take a side street so I don't have to drive past Talico Bar. Amidst the horror show that was my trip to the library, I managed to find out that Crusty has owned the dump he calls a rental property for over twenty-five years. That means B's family would have been tenants of his. While I don't relish the idea of talking to him, I have to speak to Crusty about Mom's house anyway so I'll kill two birds with one stone and have him divulge the name of his former tenants. Just not right now. I've had enough human interaction for one day and the easiest way to show

Crusty I mean business when it comes to him agreeing to put a new roof on Mom's house is by having a face-to-face conversation with the man.

Last I knew, he lived in a double-wide behind the bar. Even if I could catch him at home instead of in the bar, with the way I'm feeling right now, I'm liable to go ahead and walk into the bar anyway, and there aren't enough strangers in this town for me to start drinking. Especially in Mom's old stomping ground. I'd end up in a bed she's been in before, and if Crusty's would happen to be the one I found myself crawling out of, I'd then have to walk myself down to the railroad tracks and throw myself in front of a train.

I wind through partially deserted streets and head back toward Mom's house. I've been gone long enough that her temper should be reset. I'll feed her dinner and then spend the rest of the night scrubbing the upstairs bathroom the way I scrubbed hers yesterday. She can either go to bed or keep watching her movie because too much time has passed for us to heal our past. Years have been lost to the ravages of brokenness. Both mine and hers. There's no point in making a last-ditch effort at reconciliation now. While I'm here, I'll clean her house, feed her, keep her off the booze, and take her to all of the different doctors Aunt Di said Mom needs to see. I'll do my best to be civil while having zero expectations that she'll ever even speak to me as if I'm a human being.

I lift the nails of my right hand over the steering wheel and check the polish. My first day back in Poca, I spent five hours scouring every inch of Mom's filthy kitchen. Aunt Diana told me the place was in bad shape so I brought cleaning supplies with me, and I'm glad those supplies included heavy-duty gloves. Otherwise, the cleaner would have eaten my polish off. If being back in this place ruins my nails again, I'm afraid I'll crumble. These nails symbolize so much for me. It isn't only about my livelihood.

It's about the strength it took to walk away, and the courage I found in the battlefields of my journey.

I rest my still-intact nails back on the steering wheel and mourn once more for the life I left in Dallas. I abandoned most of what I owned, leaving it for whoever the lucky new tenant of my apartment is. It was that or rent a storage unit and after renting this car, I didn't want to spend the extra money. So I bought one large suitcase and packed it full of clothes and toiletries, then settled my traveling nail case into the trunk beside the suitcase. Those two items alone are still more than I had when I left Poca the first time so when I leave again, at least I won't be starting completely over.

Conner's face flits through my mind and a shiver skitters through my body as I replay what happened outside the library. I don't need Mom to love me. I'm too used to her not even liking me. Conner being angry with me is a different story. The way he looked at me today was unsettling, like his eyes burned into my soul, tipping everything inside of me off balance.

I turn back onto Silver Street and pass the cemetery. Mom's driveway is blocked by a charcoal-colored crew cab truck. The windows are tinted dark and there's a camper top on the back. Behind the truck is a trailer with a big industrial lawnmower sitting on it. The kind Conner was operating today. My stomach tightens into a knot. I slow down and put my blinker on, the front end of my vehicle facing his. Conner's engine starts and his window rolls down. He pulls onto the road and stops beside me. I roll my window down, finding my voice to be stronger than I feel. "Do we have a problem, Conner? Because I'm happy to call Luke—"

"Don't you dare say his name to me." Conner's nostrils flare. "Follow me, and don't think about doing anything else or I swear, Sierra, I'll make you wish you never met me."

My eyes widen. "I kind of already do. You're acting like…" My words trail off because he's acting like I betrayed him and in a way, I guess I did.

His teeth grind. "Exactly. And it's going to get a whole heck of a lot worse because you're the one person who was never supposed to step foot in this godforsaken town again. But here you are, so turn your car around and follow me."

He drives off, the lawnmower rattling behind him. I look over at Mom's graying old house with the dark shutters that are cracked and hanging loose. I could go in there and keep to my original plan but it's honestly a toss-up on what her mood will be. I already know what Conner's is, so I might as well let him get all of his frustration out now. Then maybe I can get my nerves under control and stop shaking.

~ 4 ~

Conner's genetic lottery win made him a natural for the *in* crowd. Superstar athlete on both the football and basketball teams, his athletic prowess was accompanied by a tall, muscular build, dark hair, and striking blue eyes. The too cute boy never even had a gangly stage like most of the other kids. Conner was hot from the jump and *everyone* had a crush on him.

I wish I'd felt special about the fact that he chose me, but I was sure he only did because I was conveniently right next door and didn't have a parent to get in our way. I also never put demands on him. I didn't have expectations the way other girls did. Sometimes his teammates would complain that their girlfriends were mad because they weren't getting as much attention as they wanted. Conner never had to worry about that with me. Between school and sports, he was busy. And when he wasn't, I was dutifully right next door.

I U-turn and follow him back down the road I just drove up. I might not have been his best choice, but he's the one who asked *me* to be official with him. I never demanded a label or even insisted that he acknowledge my existence when he was with his friends. He's the one who made an issue out of me being his girlfriend, and if he thinks that now gives him the right to speak to me the way he has, he's sorely mistaken. I might be more like my mother than I'm willing to admit to anyone, but I'm not trash.

Conner turns out the dirt road to the old cemetery and a pit opens up in my stomach. We came here a few times as kids. Conner said I liked making out in the creepy places, but I didn't. I never bothered correcting him, though. When he made statements about what I did or didn't like, I accepted whatever he said and when that landed me in places like this, I kept my focus on him. I was good at going through the motions. Rolling with whatever situation I found myself in, keeping the peace as best as I could while hearing and seeing what was happening around me, and all too often not recognizing the placating words coming out of my own mouth. When it came to Conner, my desire to please him nullified every other instinct. I was too weak to voice my own feelings to anyone, especially him. I guess that makes me the coward Mom said I was. But I'm not a child anymore and I deserve respect. From her, and from him.

Conner drives around the side of the cemetery, following old tracks in the grass until his truck is spun around and faces back toward the entrance again. I'm not hauling anything so I don't have to swing wide. I wait for him to shift into park and then pull up alongside him, facing into the graveyard. It's best if neither of us gets out of our vehicles. Whatever he has to say to me can be done from here. I look up at him. His truck is tall enough that my window is next to the solid steel of his door. One he can't open without dinging the side of my rental. "Here I am, Conner.

Say whatever it is you feel like you need to say. Just try to do it with a civil tone because I've had enough of you yelling at me."

His brow draws over his squinted eyes, the depth of the blue looking more like a thunderstorm than the pools of deep ocean I remember. "We had a deal."

I swallow. "Yeah, I know, and I'm sorry things ended like they did. I shouldn't have—"

"Damn right, you shouldn't have!" he shouts.

My body involuntarily flinches. I curl my fingers around the steering wheel, steadying my hands. "What's done is done, yelling about it now won't change the past." I meet his glare head-on. "I'm sorry, Conner. I'm *really* sorry."

He snorts, leaning back in his seat and dragging one of his big hands down his face. "Sorry? You thought you'd just waltz back into Poca and say you're sorry, then everything would be fine?"

I follow his lead and lean into the soft leather of my seat. "No, Conner, I didn't come here thinking I could say anything to you that would make a difference. I didn't even know if you would still be in Poca."

He groans. "Where the hell else would I be?"

I gulp against the emotion rising up my throat. I have no idea who this person is and seeing what's become of Conner hurts the tender part of me that has always been his. "You had scholarship offers. You could have taken any of those and gotten out of this town in a heck of better way than I did."

He leans out his window, angling himself down closer to me. "Yeah, I could have. But you screwed that all to hell for me just like you ruined every other damn thing in my life. And now you roll back in here like you didn't do a damn thing wrong? No. This is not happening, Sierra. Get the hell out of Poca. Tonight. And this time, stay gone."

I swipe at my eyes, lowering my head so he can't see the tears that are refusing to stay inside of me. Birds are singing from the trees around us, as if this is just another beautiful day in their world. From my perspective, this is one of the worst, because in the years I've been gone from Poca, whenever I was at my lowest, I closed my eyes and thought of Conner. His memories got me through all of the things I couldn't survive on my own. Now, all of that is gone. Conner hates me, and seeing it on his face will overshadow every other memory.

His hand stretches across the gap between our vehicles, palm resting on the top of where my window is rolled down. "Sierra, look at me." His voice is low. Soft. His fingers ticking as if he wants to touch me.

I lift my watery gaze to his, ashamed of my tears but more ashamed of what I've lived through since I saw him last. "I know I hurt you, Conner. But you're acting like what happened didn't devastate me. I'm the one who…" A tear slides down my face and he moves to wipe it away. I lean away from his touch. "I'm used to being alone in the world. I can take care of my own tears."

He rests his hand back on the window. "You're not alone, Sierra. You never have been. I just…" His throat bobs. "I can't look at you without seeing all of the things I've spent a decade trying to forget."

I lift the collar of my shirt and use it to wipe my face. "That's the difference between us, Conner. I've spent the last decade trying to remember everything about you. Because I didn't think I would ever see you again, and I never wanted to forget the time we had together."

He pulls his hand back inside his truck, straightening in his seat. "You weren't supposed to ever see me again and I sure as heck never expected you to come back here. Once you were gone, you were supposed to be gone for good."

I face forward, staring out my windshield the way he's now staring out his. This conversation is the closure we needed. Everything between us is dead now. "Believe me, Poca is the last place I ever thought I'd step foot in again, but I've stayed in contact with my aunt Di. Not a lot. I checked in with her a few times is all, but she called me recently and said that my mom was probably going to die soon, especially if she didn't get help."

He groans again. "You didn't come back for that witch so cut the crap."

I start my car. "I did come back for her. You know more than anyone that Mom doesn't deserve my help and that she wouldn't do the same for me, but she did give birth to me so I think I might owe her something."

He looks down at me. The tears are freely flowing now but he doesn't seem to care. His head shakes, as if he can't figure out what he's even looking at. "You could have decorated your bedroom with cocaine and condoms and *if* your mom would have noticed, she wouldn't have cared. This stupid obligation you feel to help her when she's never been willing to help herself should have ended when you left."

What he's saying isn't wrong. More than anyone else, Conner knows the abuse I suffered at the hands of my mom. The only parts I ever hid from him were what Mom allowed to happen whenever she decided to shack up with someone. I much preferred finding her passed out in a ditch than waking up to find some naked man sprawled on the living room couch. Half of them never had the decency to cover themselves. If they paid me any attention at all, it was the bad kind. They either hit me the way they hit Mom, or they'd tell me I was special, touching my hair and shoulders and pretending they weren't the creeps they were. I would run to Conner's when he was home. When he wasn't, I'd just hang out up on the railroad tracks that wound down the mountain behind the trailer court. None of the men ever stuck around the trailer for long and when they left, Mom always blamed me. "I can't help how I feel, Conner. If Mom had someone else, I'd leave her care to them but she's gotten too bad for Aunt Di to handle. So here I am."

He starts his own engine and shifts into gear, muttering words I can't hear over the roar of his truck as he hits the gas and drives away from me. I guess we're even now. I left him without saying goodbye and now he's returning the favor. I swing the front end of my car around and drive through the dust he's leaving behind. When we reach the end of the road, his truck turns right, the large commercial lawnmower fading in the powdery spray of earth he kicked up when he spun out onto the pavement. My insides knot and writhe, clenching and loosening as I tamp down the part of me that wants to race after him.

I turn left, away from Conner and back toward Mom's house. I broke our teenage pact so he can choose to hate me for that if he wants to. That's his right. It's also his right not to see my side of things. If he can't understand why I stole away like a thief in the night, nothing I say now will make a bit of difference.

I make a slow approach to Mom's house, attention drawn to the deep-eaved dormers that seem to watch me. I pull into the driveway and look up at the steep pitch of the hipped roof. There's a threatening quality to this house, the sharp angles unfriendly. There was a television show I used to watch where the host described haunted objects, things that held remnants of energy, both good and bad. That energy came from the living. Either their nature or their deeds. In this case, I'm sure

Mom's temperament has infected the whole structure. It's as decayed as she is, and not all of that is Crusty's fault.

~ 5 ~

June 30, 2012

I saw her tonight. My sisters didn't want me to. They had the nerve to try and hide what was happening right in front of my eyes, but it didn't work. I saw the bimbo whose smile is too wide for her face. She flirted with my boyfriend all night, touching him and laughing even when he didn't say anything funny. She all but crawled onto his lap when her stupid brother set off a string of firecrackers.

I stood in the shadows and watched them together, the bimbo and the cheat. Well, the bimbo. My sisters say that my boyfriend didn't do anything wrong. Maybe he didn't, but just because he wasn't sticking his tongue down the bimbo's throat doesn't mean he didn't want to. Her skirt was short, just like the ones she wears at the football games when she's out there cheering for the stupid high school team. I guess that's why I left the party and torched the school. Her locker was ground zero for a beautiful blaze that crawled out of the girl's locker room and lit up the sky for miles around.

When the light begins to change...

B.

I drop the diary. I remember the fire. Rumors spread all over town that summer, the cheerleaders being blamed because they'd been using the gym to run a day camp for younger girls hoping to make the cheer squad once they reached high school. People joked that curling irons and hairspray were the cause of the fire.

To my knowledge, no one person was ever charged. The whole incident was chalked up to being a devastating accident, and the cheerleaders weathered the harassment they received by doing community service. They even donned overalls and steel-toed boots to help clean up what the fire destroyed. Crews worked on the building all summer in order to have just the least damaged portion of the school ready for the new year in the fall. Trailers were brought in to supplement the classrooms and a portion of the cafeteria was walled off and used as a makeshift gym on days when the weather wasn't nice enough to be outside.

I grab my keys off the rickety dresser beside my bedroom door and take the steps two at a time. I put Mom to bed hours ago and I don't expect her to wake again until morning. This is a perfect time to visit her old buddy, especially now that it's imperative that I find out who lived in this house before Crusty rented it to Mom. I don't know if there's a statute of limitations on arson, but someone could have died in that fire, and a person willing to torch a school is a person who doesn't need to be walking among the rest of us.

I throw open the front door, my eye catching on the glint of moonlight reflecting off an object in the otherwise dark front yard. The porch light is blown. I put a new bulb in it yesterday but the whole thing exploded the second I flipped the switch. Which added having the wiring checked to my long list of items Crusty needs to address.

I pick my way down the steps and toward the silver shaft of what looks to be a cane. One exactly like Mom's. I reach down and pick it up, inspecting the dent two inches down from the handle. The ding confirms it is hers, but why is it out here? *How* did it get out here? The woman can barely walk from her bed to the toilet that adjoins her room.

I look around the wide expanse of the front yard. Where most older homes sit close to the road, this one sits farther back on its lot, making for more of a front yard than a back one. Something moves in the shadows by the road. I walk toward it cautiously, the robe-clad figure coming into focus with each step I take. Mom is face down on the ground, the tips of her fingers scratching at the road. The closer I get, the faster she claws her way forward. "Get away!" she screams. "Get away from me!"

I kneel beside her. "I would, but even if I left you out here all night, you wouldn't make it to the bar. I doubt anyone in this town would even feel sorry enough for you to pick you up and give you a ride." I brush her hair away from her dirty face. Now that I'm beside her, I can see how red and swollen it is. She's been out here for a while, clawing her way across the lawn, tears of desperation rolling down her cheeks. "I can't leave you out here, Mom, so come on, let's get you inside before someone runs you over."

~

I haven't seen Mom's combative side in so many years that I either forgot how bad it can be, or the forced sobriety is turning her into a schizophrenic with the ability to conjure the strength of ten men. No matter how much I pleaded with her, she forced me to drag, tug, lift, and shoulder the weight of her all the way back into the house while she kicked, clawed, punched, and screamed profanities. She called me every name but my given one, and by the time we reached her bedroom, she was coated in the blood she coaxed from my arms.

I pull into the newly asphalted lot in front of Talico Bar. This place was never much to look at but Crusty is certainly taking better care of his business than he is of his rental property. The building even has new siding, and this parking lot is wider than it was back when I was too young to go inside and drag Mom out of there.

I park under the glow of a streetlight and pull the sleeves of my sweatshirt up, inspecting the gouges Mom's nails dug into my skin. To keep this from happening again, I'll have to talk her into letting me give her a manicure so I can file her nails down to nothing. The only way I even got her to quiet down tonight was by promising her alcohol. The woman was so excited for it that she didn't even balk when the promised alcohol came in the form of cough syrup. She drank it down greedily, licking the cup clean before lying down on her side and curling up into a ball like a child. It was if she hadn't just been screaming so loudly that we're lucky the neighbors didn't call the police.

I tug my sleeves back down and step out of the car, praying the wounds don't start bleeding again and that the fabric of my sweatshirt doesn't ride up past my wrists while I'm inside hunting Crusty. He'll either be in the bar or out back in his double-wide. The parking lot is fuller than I expected it to be on a Thursday night, so my guess is that I'll find him in the bar.

I move toward the two large doors that form the entrance, pausing in the mix of country music and murmuring voices spilling out of the dimly lit establishment. I'm not here to impress anyone and I sure as heck don't want a date with anyone in this town, but there's bound to be people I know inside. I look down at my tennis shoe-clad feet sticking out from under the frayed hem of my jeans. I can't say I was thinking about anything other than finding clean clothes when I washed up and changed into my current attire after Mom attacked me. My only clear thoughts were to find long sleeves and make sure that dose of cough syrup did its job. After confirming Mom was sound asleep, I left the house without considering the fact that I was heading to one of the only bars in Poca.

I brush a hand through my hair and look around at the other vehicles. Some of them probably belong to people I went to school with. Ones I wasn't friends with because while most of what I had to say about my mom wasn't nice, what the other kids said was cruel. They acted as if their assessment of her applied to me as well. That's what made it so hard for me to be Conner's plus one.

The situation couldn't have been fun for him either. The girls in the group Conner hung out with would plan shopping trips and spa days right in front of me, talking up what a fun day it was going to be while completely exiling me from the conversation. I was always the odd man out. The person who didn't fit in anywhere because no one but Conner wanted me to.

Now I'm back here among them, dressed like a slob and giving them every reason to believe I'm the trailer trash they professed me to be. They might have overlooked where Conner came from but they made sure I didn't ever forget it. So as embarrassing as it is to run into people looking the way I do, the alternative would be equally embarrassing. I'd rather look as if I'm not trying than waltz into the bar dressed to impress people I wouldn't talk to even if I did impress them. They don't know me and I don't want them to, so I won't make the mistake I made with Jan. I won't name drop or talk up my life. These leeches can keep right on thinking the worst of me.

I steel my nerves and march to the doors, shoving them open and walking in with confidence that will fade if I stay here too long. I shoot a quick glance around the place, locating my target off to the right. Crusty is behind the bar managing to hold a cigarette in his mouth while he animatedly tells a story to a couple of men sipping on mugs of freshly poured beer. Behind them on the wall is a large K crusted with glitter. It's so out of place that I can't help but stare at it.

Crusty and his entourage laugh, snapping me out of the K's trance. I give my head a little shake. I have no idea why Poca has suddenly adopted the letter K as a mascot but I'm seeing the letter everywhere. Store windows, telephone poles, and even the tin one hanging from the library's front door.

I put away my curiosity and focus my attention back on Crusty. Between the liquor and the rent, every cent of Mom's disability check has gone to him for years. It's high time he steps up as a landlord.

~6~

I'm directly in Crusty's line of sight as I approach the bar. The two men he was talking to before falling silent in the wake of my approach turn to see what he's staring at. The man on the right wipes foam off his upper lip as he gives me a once-over. I shudder. I can't be certain, but he looks like the man who used to drive through the trailer park checking meters for the water company. I saw him leaving our trailer once when I was on my way home from school. I know for a fact Mom didn't have the cash to pay the water bill that month, but it was never shut off. The man must have gotten his money's worth.

I once again force my focus back on Crusty, the shot glass in his hand stilled midway to his mouth. "Hi, Rusty." I soften my expression. This, and me using his real name, is as much kindness as he'll get from me. A smile is something I'll never offer him. "Can I talk to you for a minute?"

His lips turn up in a wicked grin and he throws the shot back, smacking his lips as the liquid burns down his throat. "Anything as pretty as you can talk to me anytime. Want to grab a bottle of Jack and follow me out to my place?"

My body tenses, hands tightening into fists. If he didn't make the offer sound so lewd, and right in front of everyone, I would say yes. Speaking to him in private would be better than doing this here. "I asked to have a word with you, I didn't offer to screw you in exchange for an open bar tab." The words fall out of my mouth, loose and angry, like I have no control over my lips. I'm usually better at keeping my thoughts inside but being back in Poca is doing strange things to my psyche.

Crusty and his two buddies laugh as if I'm an amusing little girl. Despite the rage burning in my chest, I sedately nod to a private spot near the opposite end of the bar. "I can talk to you just fine over there."

Crusty sweeps an arm in the direction I indicated. "Go ahead, beautiful. Your first drink is on me."

"Right out of his lint-filled belly button," the second man snickers, setting the three of them and several other bystanders to laughter again.

I walk away and wait at the end of the bar, sliding onto a sticky barstool that's going to make me have to trash these pants when I leave here. Crusty leans his elbows onto the bar top in front of me, and I've never been so glad to have a counter between us. "What can I do for you, sweet thing?"

I narrow my eyes. "For starters, you can stop calling me pet names."

He chuckles. "You can't blame an old man for trying. You're just about prettier than anything we ever get in here."

My anger rises a level. To the point that my vision is going dark. If Crusty keeps this up, it won't be long before all I see is red. I'm already half on my way to throat punching him. "I'm Wanda's daughter. Sierra."

His eyes dip to my chest, scanning my completely covered up breasts. "I know who you are. You're a little more filled out than the last time I saw you but you're not fooling anyone in that getup. You've still got a sexy little girlish figure." His eyes meet mine. "And now you're legal."

I bristle, venomous words dripping from my lips. "And you're one syllable away from me ripping out that disgusting tongue of yours and shoving it up your..." I clamp my mouth shut and lean away from him. The ordeal with Mom must have drained every drop of patience I have and replaced it with pure rage. I've never in my life spoken to someone this way. That's part of why I left Poca in the first place. I was tired of being passive, but I also didn't want to be a mean and cynical person. In Poca, those were my only two options. Outside of this place, I got to be exactly who I am.

Crusty's eyes narrow, scanning mine like I'm a peon who has no right to speak to him at all, let alone the way I just did. Fair enough. On the no right to speak to him that way part. I clear my throat. "I'm sorry. I've had a really bad day, but that's no reason to take it out on you." The apology is bitter on my tongue, making me consider if my tongue is the one that should be ripped out.

Crusty slowly pulls his elbows off the counter and straightens, standing tall with his shoulders squared to me. He's trying to intimidate me. I huff out a breath, squaring my own shoulders to let him know his antics aren't working. "Look, I'm not here to drink, flirt, or fight. So you can stop testing the waters because I'm not my mom. In fact, there's not much I have in common with Wanda, but I am here to talk about her. The shack you're renting to her is falling down. If you're going to take her money, then you're going to fix the house. The roof, the wiring, the mold... All of it."

He leans back onto the bar. "Wanda's got one of the biggest houses in the county, and for what I'm charging her, she's practically living there rent-free. She knew when she moved in that repairs would have to be paid for out of her own pocket."

I fold my arms to keep from throwing that punch into his throat. "You know as well as I do that my mom's pockets are empty. You've taken every dime she's ever stumbled her drunk self upon. So let's talk about all the violations you're facing for renting a house that's practically condemned."

He presses his lips tightly together, eyes still scanning to assess just how serious I am, and no doubt what it's going to take for him to break me. I unfold my arms and place them gently on the bar in front of me, keeping a safe distance from his ugly face but leaning toward it nonetheless. He needs to understand the severity of this situation. "I'm not here to cause trouble for you, but if I have to, I will burn down everything around you because the condition of Wanda's house is deplorable. I can't even believe you found anyone to rent it before you pawned it off on her. Who was that, by the way? What ill-advised person did you rent that dump to before Wanda?"

His cheeks puff, a disgusted snarl twisting out of him. "Like I said, that place is one of the biggest houses in the county and *everyone* I rent to knows they have to do their own fixin'. Your mom agreed to it the same way Ethel Wycamp did."

"Wycamp?" I ask. "That's the family who lived in your shack directly before Wanda moved into it?"

He straightens off the bar again and scratches his jaw, the graying beard patchy on his dry skin. His nose is bulbous and red. All signs that the alcohol hasn't been good to him either. "No. Ethel is who I rented to, because she needed a *nice* place for her niece to live. Ethel paid, and Heather lived there. And neither of them ever complained about a dang thing."

I press out a mocking laugh. "If Ethel Wycamp holed her niece up in your dump, then she sure must have hated Heather. Who else did Ethel hate? Did Heather have sisters? Or any other family forced to live there with her?"

Crusty steps away from the bar and taps his temple. "The only thing that gal had was a problem with her head. Slow. Kind of quiet and well, just plain old dumb."

"So she acts like you then?" I resist the urge to slap a hand over my mouth. I normally tend not to even ask questions, let alone spit out saucy, hate-filled comments. A product of having a parent who'd rather backhand me than tell me a single truth. When I talked back to Mom, she wasn't ever gentle in her punishment. After a few broken teeth that I had to lie to the dentist about, I learned to keep my mouth shut.

Crusty points at me. "You sure are judgy and expecting a lot for someone who hasn't spent a dime in my bar."

I tip my body away from him and dig a five-dollar bill out of my pocket. "So much for that free drink then?" I toss the money onto the counter. "My mom has spent enough in here that I'm owed some answers, but just to be nice, I'll take a bottle of your cheapest beer."

He swipes the money from the counter and shuffles over to a cooler that's stashed underneath the bar. He pops the top off a bottle and slides it down the bar to me. "Tastes like you're chewing on pickled tree bark but you get what you pay for."

I wrap my fingers around the bottle and don't bother taking a drink. "You can keep the four dollars in change then."

He smirks, then hollers at his friends down on the other end of the bar. "Hey, what was the name of Heather's boy? That spindly kid who was all elbows and big feet."

The water man bounces a finger in the air, his head nodding along. "Oh yeah, I remember that kid. Brian, wasn't it?"

My breath catches. "Brian?"

Crusty comes back to my end of the bar. "Yeah, that was his name. Brian. Why? You thinking he's going to fix up Wanda's house for you? I'd say your chances with that are about as good as me falling for the sob story you're in here trying to sell me."

I slide my hands away from the beer like doing so will separate me from Crusty's words. I need a minute to process the information he just laid on me. I assumed B was a female but maybe I was wrong. The diary entry about standing in the shadows watching his boyfriend flirt with a girl makes sense if he, his boyfriend, or both of them, weren't *out* yet. "Did Brian have sisters?"

"Not a single one." A voice that isn't Crusty's answers, the owner of the voice sliding onto the barstool next to mine and edging their body into my personal space. I whirl toward them. Luke's smile is slow and deliberate. He settles his arm around my back. "Hey there, Sierra. I told you I'd be seeing you again."

Crusty tracks Luke's arm, shifting uncomfortably with the lawman's obvious claim to the woman he's been attempting to intimidate. Luke does his own tracking, intercepting Crusty's roaming eyes. "Go get the lady and me something worth drinking."

Crusty moves off with a huff. I angle slightly away from Luke's side, trying not to be obvious in my discomfort over his closeness. "Thanks, Luke. Creepy Crusty is worse than I remember."

Luke grins, slipping his arm from behind me to let me know he appreciates why I angled away from his embrace. "I don't remember that being his name but it's fitting. He certainly likes to creep on the ladies and I've seen the inside of his double-wide. Crusty for sure."

I shrug. "It can't be worse than the investment property he's letting rot into the ground."

Luke slides the disgusting bottle of beer Crusty served me over to the empty stool beside him. "Living in your mom's place has to be better than forcing that liquid down your throat."

I snort. "Only if you don't believe living knee-deep in mold is dangerous."

Luke's golden eyebrows hit his equally golden hairline. "Seriously? I haven't been inside that place in years but it wasn't so bad before."

Crusty slams two glasses of froth-topped beer in front of us. "If that house is full of mold, it's because Wanda hasn't done anything about it. When she asked to rent that house I made a solid deal with her. You remember that, Sierra. *She* asked *me* if she could rent that house, not the other way around, and *she* said she'd take care of the repairs."

I pick up my mug of beer and take a sip. I can't challenge him about my mom being the one begging to rent that dump from him because I'm sure she did, and without being the least bit curious as to the water damage or what it would take to fix it. The only way that rotten roof would get her attention is if it were leaking liquor. "I don't care what agreement you made with a drunk. Between the rent and the liquor, all of Wanda's money has gone straight to you for years. There's also a little thing called tenant's rights." He opens his mouth but I slam my mug down, splashing booze all over his counter. "I'm not arguing about this, I'm telling you. Fix the house. It's a lot worse than when Heather lived there. When did you say she moved out?"

He glances from me to Luke and back again, annoyance coating his voice. "About a year or so before your mother *asked* to move into that house with a *discounted* rate so she could *fix it herself*."

Luke slides his stool back and throws a twenty on the counter. "That's enough, Donahue. If Sierra says your house is a dump, it is. Get the roof replaced before I send code enforcement out to take a look at the whole place." He slips my mug from the counter and picks up his own, nodding for me to follow him. "Let's find ourselves a table."

Crusty shakes his head, as if he can't believe Luke is on my side. I give him one last long look. I'm normally nonconfrontational but this place is making me crazy, so I lean into what I'm feeling in my bones and grab the bad bottle of beer from where Luke put it. I shove it across the bar to Crusty. "This beer is less toxic than the house my mom is living in. Drink up, and then let me know when the roof is being repaired."

Luke chuckles and I turn away from the bar, following him as he slips through the crowd, weaving in and out of pockets of people whose faces I refuse to look at. Crusty wasn't attempting to keep all of our conversation private and even now, I can hear him talking about me to the men at the other end of the bar, the three of them snickering. It feels like I'm back in middle school with everyone around me staring and whispering.

Luke settles on a high-top table and plops our mugs down, stealing a chair from the next table over and holding it for me. "Here we are, my feisty lady."

I shudder, sitting down and wrapping my hand around the mug as if it can give me some form of moral support. "I'm hardly feisty. Poca just brings out the worst in me, I guess."

Luke tugs his chair as close to mine as possible and sits down with a wide grin on his sun-kissed face. "I'm glad this town is forcing you to speak up. When you lived here before, you were as quiet as the day is long." He takes a sip of his beer and folds his arm along the back of my chair. "I hated not hearing your pretty voice."

I roll my eyes and then offer him a small smile, trying to hide a severe case of nerves that's causing my hands to shake. Now that I'm away from the confrontation with Crusty, I'm coming down off the high of whatever was driving me to be strong in the face of a man like that.

Despite Luke paying me a strange sort of compliment, the jitters are coming on strong. "When was the last time you were in my mom's house?"

His fingers brush my shoulder and I take a big gulp of my beer, shifting a little forward when I do. He ends the caress and takes a sip of his own beer. "It's been a number of years. I don't recall exactly but I haven't been inside that house since Heather lived there, so like I said, quite a number of years."

That means he was a teenager the last time he was in Mom's house. I draw in a steady breath, hoping to seem nonchalant with my question. "Were you friends with Heather's son? What was his name again? Brian?"

Luke's face darkens. "I don't know if I would call us friends, but I did hang out with him some. He was a sweet kid."

His choice of words spins the wheels of my curiosity even more. I only ever knew Luke to date females but if he was secretly Brian's boyfriend, that would fit with the whole closeted lover scenario. I can't come right out and ask him that, though. Can I? "Crusty said Brian's mom was a little off, like maybe she was slow or something?"

Luke swallows, his Adam's apple bobbing. "She was. Brian, too. That's why he didn't go to school with us. He had some sort of homeschooling with online classes catered to a person with his needs."

I study Luke's profile, his eyes focused on the liquid in his mug. "You sure do know a lot about Brian. Maybe you were more than just friends?"

Luke swipes at the building perspiration on his forehead. "More than friends?" He meets my eyes. "I'm attracted to women, Sierra, if that's what you're getting at."

I place my hand on his leg to reassure him. "Sometimes people are attracted to both, and that's okay. I'm just curious about Brian and maybe who he was interested in, male or female."

Luke slides his hand down to his leg and covers my hand, leaning in closer like he has a secret to tell. He runs his finger around the lobe of my ear, tucking the hair away as he whispers. "I'm pretty sure he liked girls, they just didn't like him. Sometimes I have that same problem. Like right now, when the female I'm trying to hit on suddenly thinks I'm batting for the other team. How can I prove I'm not?"

My cheeks heat and I bite my lip. Truth be told, the last male who outright flirted with me was Conner. Since then, I've been easy pickings. The men around me could smell the blood in the water, circling me with little attempt at hiding their true intentions. They'd give me a ride if I'd give them one. Even now, when I don't need anything from a man, I don't get hit on by decent ones who want to get to know me. I guess that's why I let my loneliness reach desperate levels before going the bender and strangers for bedmates route. Luke isn't a stranger, though, and the last time I sat this close to a man, I had a mug of beer in my hand a lot like the one I'm sipping now. That particular series of snapshots isn't a memory I want to relive. So despite how good Luke's hand feels cupped over mine, I do *not* want to encourage him. In fact, I should run out the door right now. I slip my hand from underneath his. "Um, was Brian *off* enough to get mad if someone didn't return his affection?"

Luke's face falls, like I've just sucked all the effort out of him and tossed it away. He takes a long drink of his beer, setting it back down and keeping his eyes trained on it. "No, I wouldn't peg him for the angry rejected sort, but I also don't actually know a lot about the kid. What I've already told you is about all I know. So now you answer my question. Why are you so concerned about Brian? Did you even know him?"

I shake my head and follow Luke's lead in swallowing down a gulp of beer, buying time to answer him as the decision whether or not to tell him about the diary weighs and tears. He's a cop, and it would be nice to have someone to talk to about B, but there's a swirling in my gut that says Luke is not the right person. Especially if he secretly was dating Brian. "As small as Poca is, I really only knew the kids in our grade and the people who lived around me in the trailer court. I'm using the term *knew* loosely, because I really didn't talk to anyone much, as you pointed out earlier."

Luke leans against the back of his chair and moves his arm up around my shoulders, pulling me into his side. "Life sucked for both of us back then. Neither of us had a real family. All we had at home was misery. That's why we always got along like we did. Misery recognizes misery. Even without telling you what was going on in my life, I felt like you understood. Like you saw me."

I stare at him wide-eyed and gape-mouthed. His description of the bond we had is accurate, only I had no idea it was because Luke was as miserable as I was. He wasn't as jovial as Conner but he was still a go-lucky sort. I heard stories about his stepdad using his position as a policeman to take advantage of people, especially women, but that information mostly came from Conner. He told me that if I was alone and Luke's stepdad came around, I should run. One time when Conner let me borrow his car while he was at football practice, Gerald Putnam pulled me over. When I told Conner about it later his face had frozen until I got to the part where I didn't pull over until I reached the very public supermarket parking lot. "Your stepdad abused you?"

Luke tightens his hold and tucks me in closer, our faces inches apart. "No one knew the full extent of the things he used to do, just like I doubt anyone knew the full extent of what your mom put you through. But I can imagine what those things might have been," he whispers. "I was only in Heather's house because my stepdad used to *visit* her. He'd make me go there with him, to keep Brian occupied while he..."

His sentence finishes in my mind and my heart squeezes. I wrap a fist in Luke's soft blue t-shirt. "I'm so sorry. I knew he wasn't a good person but I didn't realize he treated his family so terribly. It must have been awful to be in that house knowing what he was doing."

Luke lifts a hand to my face. "It was. But dang if I didn't forget about it every time I saw you."

Sorrow filters through me. Luke recognized my pain but I didn't see his because my own was too raw. All I recognized was that I felt a sense of acceptance when Luke was around. The only other person who ever comforted me that way was Conner, and my relationship with him was so much more than anything I ever had with Luke. "Misery is a crummy reason for us to be friends but yeah, I felt like you saw me too, and you didn't mind all the bad parts. At least not enough to completely isolate me."

He presses a kiss to my forehead. "I never saw any bad parts. I'm fairly certain you don't have any. In fact, you're so darn perfect I'm as blinded by looking at you now as I was back then."

I laugh. "Well, Crusty did say I'm *almost* as pretty as anything that ever comes into his bar, so I guess I'm doing something right. Or the rest of the women in Poca know not to come in here."

Luke glances toward the bar. "I knew when I saw him leering at you the way he was, I should arrest him. Creepy old man. I can't have him on the loose telling lies, and that's what he was doing because I can personally vouch for you being *the* prettiest thing this bar has ever seen."

I cock an eyebrow. "That makes it sound like you come here a lot. So are you an aspiring alcoholic? Or looking for one to date? From personal experience, I can vouch for alcoholism not being the ticket to happiness."

His head shakes and a laugh spills over his lips. "You caught me. Truth is, I don't get out much and it's been a while since I've had to do this. Which is why my flirting game is terrible." He looks down at me. "I just called you a *thing* instead of a woman. Will it do any good if I start backpedaling and try to correct all the wrong things I've said, or will I only be sticking my foot in my mouth deeper?"

I run my finger down his Adam's apple. "Deeper."

His eyes heat and pinpricks race up my spine. I can't tell if they're good or bad, or why in the heck I very clearly just made an innuendo. I lean out of his arms and pick up my mug, draining the glass and letting the liquid settle in my stomach before I look back at him. Maybe spending a night with him wouldn't be so bad after all. "All joking aside, what brings you into a bar like this one on a Thursday night? I find it hard to believe that Luke Putnam doesn't have a girlfriend or even a wife waiting for him at home." A shadow falls over his features. He picks up his mug and downs it the way I just did with mine. I raise a brow. "That bad, huh?"

He plops the empty glass back down, a heavy sigh rattling his chest. "I was married. *Am* married," he corrects, tugging me back into his embrace with an easy grin sliding onto his face. "Getting divorced. The paperwork is filed, we just haven't finalized it yet. And I've been feeling pretty blue about it all until I saw you." He looks at his watch. "About darn time you rolled back into town. I've been waiting on you since middle school."

My eyes fling open and he shakes his head in disbelief. "Don't act so surprised. I never hid my crush on you, I just didn't have any game back then. Or now either, apparently. But in eighth grade, when you wore that pink dress to the snowball dance, I was so sure I was going to get words to come out of my mouth so that I could dance with you, that I turned down Hilary when she asked me to dance. I told her I had a girlfriend. Then I chickened out on actually making that dream come true. After trying to ask you to dance with me about forty-five times in a row, I gave up and called my mom to come get me."

I cover my mouth, trying not to laugh. I fail. He fake glares at me. "Thanks for the compassion."

I lower my hand. "I'm sorry. But are you messing with me right now? How on earth can you remember what I wore to a dance in eighth grade?"

He drops his arm from my shoulders and slides it down my back, his hand resting on my hip. "I remember the dress, the shoes, your hair..." His lips press against my ear. "And how much I hoped to get a kiss out of you that night. I didn't have any luck, but maybe tonight I'll do a little better. Will you dance with me, Sierra?"

I created what I told myself was a full life in Dallas, but Luke's presence tonight is a wake-up call. I might not have had many friends in Poca, only two really, but in Dallas I have none. I have acquaintances. People I don't hang out with after hours or talk to about my life. Though free to live however I want, what I surrounded myself with is loneliness. Luke is reminding me that I don't want to be lonely anymore.

His eyes twinkle and I can't help but smile back at him. He shoves his chair back and pulls me to my feet, the corners of his eyes crinkling as his smile spreads wide across his face. "All roads brought us here, to you dancing with me in this bar neither of us likes."

I laugh as he spins me out and around the tiny patch of floor beside our table, bringing me back to his chest with a quick snap of his wrist. Another laugh bubbles out of me. "You lied to me, Luke. Your flirting skills aren't rusty at all."

"Good." He pulls me close, one hand holding mine and the other resting low on my back.

A huge chunk of me likes where this is going, but the rest of me is screaming that Luke is not whose bed I want to wake up in. He isn't a stranger and he isn't a one-night stand. He also can't be a full-blown relationship. I don't plan on being in Poca long enough for that, and besides, *getting* divorced doesn't mean he's free. This man whose arms I'm enjoying is technically married. "How long have you been separated?"

"Not long." He pushes me out and twirls me into a dip, then lifts me up and brings me back into his arms. "I've had a lot of time to think about what I might say to you if I ever saw you again, and I've not kept on script at all tonight."

I curl my arm around his neck. From how I'm pressed against him, I can feel that he's taut, his body lined with muscle that my fingers are set on exploring. "Nice way to change the subject, but if you're going to make me believe you've spent years pining, you're going to have to tell me about this marriage of yours. You're not even thirty yet and already getting divorced? Exactly how long have you been married, Mr. Putnam?"

He frowns. "If you must know, *Detective*, right now in this moment when I'd rather not kill the mood we're working on, I got married the summer I graduated from high school. I went to a concert over spring break and fell hard for the girl fate seated next to me. It was a whirlwind, and up until recently, I thought it was a fairly good marriage."

"What happened?" I blush, ashamed I can't stop myself from asking more questions.

He shakes his head, a grin riding his lips as he slows down our dance and rests his forehead on mine, ignoring the faster tempo of the music filling the bar. "Life happened, Sierra, and it sucked right up until the moment I saw you at the library. Now it's your turn to answer some of my questions. What happened to you? You were here one day and gone the next. People talked, but Conner wouldn't acknowledge your name, and your mom... Well, I dropped by her place a few times but she was about as helpful as Conner. I couldn't make sense of it. She didn't file a police report or put up any missing person flyers. It was like she just..."

"Didn't care?" I finish for him. "She doesn't. She was never too hands-on so when I left, that suited her just fine."

His revelation about Conner makes my head spin, my emotions conflicting with what I thought I knew and what the truth really is. Other than being mad that I left without him, it sounds like Conner was no better than my mom. They were both happy to erase me.

I rest my head on Luke's shoulder, swaying with him to a slow tune only he can hear. "I care," he whispers, arms tight in their warm embrace as he holds me close, like he knows all about the cyclone of emotion I'm navigating. I relax into him and resolve to go wherever he leads tonight. Even if it's to his bed. I deserve to be cared for and so does Luke. We can both give that to each other, if only for one single night. Or for several of them. Maybe while I'm here, we can find solace in each other's arms.

I close my eyes. The decision to sleep with him seems like it can't possibly be my own, but it is. One beer isn't clouding my judgment. I'm a long way from blacking out and for once in my adult life, I don't want to. I want to be present for this. I want to feel Luke close to me, remembering every detail, however fleeting that closeness might be.

Luke's hand rides lower and I open my eyes, set on asking him if we can get out of this bar that neither of us likes, but it isn't Luke's face I see. My gaze is fixed on a pair of searing blue eyes storming their way through the crowd. The intensity of Conner's glare burns into me. I flinch away from Luke as if he's the cause of the heat charring my flesh. He chuckles, unaware of the volcano heading our way. "Did I step on your foot?" He fits his hands on my hips and brings me back to his chest. "My dancing skills might be as bad as my flirting, but I'll get better. Now that I have the right partner."

Shouts erupt as Conner shoves a moose of a man out of his way, anger rolling off him in waves thick enough to crack a fault line through the earth beneath us. The hair on the back of my neck rises, his fury pressurizing the air around me, pushing into me, killing every mood Luke has put his time into creating for us. My dance partner finally looks to see what the commotion is all about, his body stiffening as he sees what I see. A pissed off Conner with a face full of contempt.

I tug at Luke's shirt. His easy smile is gone and he's watching every move made in Conner's thunderous approach. He shifts his stance to face the beast heading our way, sliding his body in front of mine. "Stay behind me," he orders. I lift onto my tiptoes, looking over his shoulder at the turbulent storm of a man who is now only feet away. Luke holds up a hand. "Stop right there. Sierra is here with me tonight and you need to go on your merry way."

Conner doesn't acknowledge Luke or slow down even a fraction. He's dug so deeply into my eyes that I'm not even sure he sees Luke. Panic grips me and I move to the side, darting away from Luke in order to draw Conner away from him. Luke mumbles a curse and shoots out a hand, grabbing my arm and unknowingly busting open one of Mom's gouges. Conner's big arm swings wide, his palm cupping the whole side of Luke's face as he knocks Luke off balance and throws him away from me. His other hand clamps onto my wrist, his grip gentler than his demeanor lets on, yet still firm enough that I can't escape him. "We're leaving," he growls.

Luke rights himself and rushes to my side, a trickle of blood on the corner of his lip. He's not backing down even though Conner is taller and his shoulders broader. He shoves in front of me, meeting Conner chest-to-chest, forcing Conner to release his grip on me. The two men square up and I scramble around Luke, trying to shove myself between them before this turns into a full-on fistfight. The bar around us is already growing silent, despite the music. Conner's warpath drew everyone's attention and it's hard to say if they'll want to break this up or egg it on. Probably depends on who has more friends in this bar and Luke being a cop, I'm guessing Conner might be the crowd favorite.

Despite my shoving, neither man is giving up an inch. Conner is no longer focused on me. His eyes are now fully trained on Luke, the icy blaze inside them full of bloodlust. "Stop it!" I shout at him.

Luke finally gives me space, stepping backward and running an arm around my waist when I rush between them. He pulls me against him, head dipping down and his lips finding my cheek. "Don't worry, sweetheart, we're going to finish our dance."

Conner's chest heaves. I thrust a hand out as he moves forward, my fingers once again pressed to his chest and trapped between us. "Stop," I beg, unsure why he's even behaving this way. He made it clear he despises the sight of me, so whatever is happening between these two men is something they're literally putting me in the middle of. To what end?

I wiggle against Luke, jabbing an elbow into his gut and stepping on his foot until he backs up enough that I can free my trapped hand and peel his arm from my waist. I step to the side and look between them, scolding between clenched teeth. "Stop this nonsense right now." Both of their heads turn in my direction. I narrow my eyes. "I will *not* be the cause of your barroom brawl."

Luke's jaw ticks. He holds his hand out to me. "You're right. Let's get out of here and find a place to dance where we won't be interrupted."

Conner doesn't offer me a hand, he reaches out and anchors his palms to my upper arms, yanking me to him and leaning down until his face is a hair's breadth from my own. "Luke is only with you because I slept with his wife. He's using you to piss me off, and succeeding at doing a hell of a lot more than that, so don't you freaking touch him again or I'll show him how beyond pissed I really am."

~*9*~

My head collides with Conner's nose. I don't care. I keep spinning until I'm facing Luke. "You're using me to make Conner jealous because he had an affair with your wife?"

Luke turns red from the neck up, his eyes darting around us before coming back to rest on me. He takes a step forward, his voice low. "That delinquent did a lot more than break up my marriage, and he'll get what's coming to him in the end, but no, Sierra, I'm not using you. He is. He's jealous and petty and he can't stand that I'm—"

Conner's fist cuts off Luke's words. Blood and spit fling from Luke's mouth. He snaps his head forward and rushes Conner, landing an uppercut as the two of them crash through a table. Conner flips Luke off of him and before my own gasp reaches my ears, bystanders are jumping into the mass of writhing limbs, the epicenter growing until I'm sure no one is breaking this up.

An errant elbow collides with my spine. I pitch forward, temple colliding with a chair beside the high-top Luke and I were sitting at earlier. I curl a protective arm around my head and look around me. More bodies are running this way. I skirt around them, ducking and weaving until I can see the door. I keep my feet moving, putting distance between myself and the brawl until I'm shoving through the doors I never should have walked through in the first place. I spill out into the night air and welcome the cool nip of the wind's embrace. The next time I need to speak to Crusty, I'll take him up on the offer to go out back to his place.

"Sierra!" Conner's shout reaches me just as I open my car door. I glance over my shoulder. He barrels through a group of people who are also trying to escape the fighting. "Sierra, wait!"

I glare at him. "Don't you mean leave? Because that's all you've been saying to me since I got here!"

He slows his pace, his movements stiff and his dark hair rumpled. "Yeah, I do want you to leave. With me. You've been drinking so I'll drive you home."

I get into the car. He lunges for the door, keeping me from closing it. I narrow my eyes. "I had *one* drink, so go back inside and gloat to Luke about breaking up his marriage *and* his date because I don't need you to do *anything* for me."

He keeps a tight grip on the door with one hand and rubs his red jaw with the other, dismissing my anger so he can keep dishing out his own. "Take your indignation down a notch because you're not deserving of it," he nips. "When I drove by here I could hardly believe I was seeing *your* car at this bar. Then I have to walk in there and see in you *Luke's* arms? Not going to happen, Sierra. Not going to freaking happen."

I start my car. "I'm certain no one forced you to walk in there and I'm even more sure that whose arms I'm in has nothing to do with you."

Conner slams his hand against the roof and lowers his face down to mine. I reach over and turn the radio up so loud that it drowns out whatever he's saying. He shouts louder. I drop the car into gear and move forward. He can either let go of the door or get himself dragged across the pavement. It's his choice.

~

Sunlight filters through my bedroom window, casting shadows along the floor and over my bed, the wind blowing the tree branches outside just enough to make dawn's light dance over my blankets and up into my eyes. I roll over with a groan. Luke's betrayal and Conner's viciousness are still too fresh in my mind for dawn to hasten me into another day. What little sleep I had was restless and my stomach feels like everything I've eaten in the last week is on the verge of coming back up.

I shove the stiff covers off of me and swing my feet to the floor. The mental stress of what happened last night has me feeling like I'm hungover, complete with a full room tilt that has me swaying before I even stand up. If it wasn't for Mom needing breakfast soon, I'd pull the blankets over my head and will myself back to sleep. I have to fix her breakfast, though, and sit beside her afterward. Otherwise, she won't eat a thing. From the lack of food in the house when I arrived, I believe Aunt Di was right about Mom not having a proper meal in a very long time. The woman is coatrack thin, clothes hanging on her in a way that's far from a fashion choice. Mom is so used to filling her belly with alcohol that she's drunk herself into an eating disorder.

I push up off the bed and steady my posture before taking a step toward the door. I've vowed to make sure Mom eats at least two decent meals a day. Breakfast and dinner. The way I figure it, breakfast is important to get her strength up for the day, although she'll spend the entirety of it sitting in front of her DVD player. For lunch, she can have any snack she might want, if she feels like her stomach can handle it. Then dinner is another proper meal she needs to eat. A full belly helps me sleep so I assume the same is true for her. Plus, I put her to bed right after I feed her so that gives her stomach the whole night to remind itself of how to process solid food.

I trek a slow pace across my room, thinking of what I can make for breakfast that requires as little effort as possible. I'm not a chef by any stretch of anyone's imagination. I taught myself the basics by watching cooking shows on a network made for the express purpose of celebrating food. My one specialty is biscuits. I make them so often that out of habit, I keep butter chunked and ready to use straight out of the freezer. Judging by the fact that Mom ate almost all of the last batch I made, I think biscuits are a safe bet for this morning. While they're baking I'll fry up some ham and scramble some eggs. First, I need a shower. There's a stench clinging to my hair that I can't quite place. That's what happens when you visit bars, the foul smell of drunks attaches itself to you.

I stumble into the tiny upstairs bathroom and turn on the shower, stripping off my clothes and stepping into the cold stream. My eyes spring open and my breath comes out in shallow bursts. I need the shock of this wake-up call but I miss the hot and hard spray of my shower back in Dallas. In this house, you have to be made of patience to get even a warm shower. By the time the hot water filters up from the tank in the basement, it's practically cold again.

The water temperature is a little better downstairs in the bathroom that was built off the side of the kitchen, but the pressure is still nonexistent and I'd rather not share a bathroom with Mom. Since she can no longer navigate the stairs, she can have the bathroom adjacent to her bedroom and I'll keep this whole top floor to myself, dated and crumbling mess that it is.

I scrub my hair clean and rinse it out as quickly as possible, turning off the icy water and throwing open the shower curtain. I pull a fresh towel off the stack of new ones I bought. I even bought the hamper I'm currently using as a shelf for said towels. Come winter, if I'm still in this rickety old house, I'm going to have to buy a space heater for this room like the one I had in here as a teen. It's already practically unbearable and July is one of the warmest months in Poca.

I dry and dress quickly, tugging sweatpants over my legs and pulling a long-sleeved cotton shirt over my head. I left these clothes in here two days ago when I made the last batch of biscuits, because anything I wear after taking an ice cold shower has to be winter wear and not Poca-in-July garb. Considering the missing flesh on my arms, it's a good thing I had the forethought to bring an ample supply of long sleeves with me. You never know how the weather is going to crawl over the mountains and settle on Poca, so I came prepared for any sudden cool spells or nightly plummeting temperatures. Little did I know that I'd also be donning this attire because of battle scars.

I stare at my reflection in the peeling mirror above the small green sink that took me half a day to scrub clean. The face looking back at me has a sour expression, as if asking me what I'm even doing here. Good question. I wish I could answer it in a way that would satisfy both of us. "It's complicated," I mutter, popping open the plastic box on the corner of the sink. I pull my toothpaste out and tug my toothbrush from the cup beside the box, wetting it before applying a generous dose of mouth-cleaning goodness. Thankfully I didn't mix spit with Luke last night but I still feel gross for even being willing to.

I begin to scrub my teeth, walking away from the sink to grab my hairbrush from beside the stack of towels. With one hand, I work a brush over my teeth while the other works a brush through my short locks. A mark on the side of the mirror where the chipped paint is peeling away from the rustic wooden frame catches my attention. I return to the sink and lean close to the mark that looks a whole lot like a K etched into the wood with a ballpoint pen. A shiver crawls up my spine. Not only is the mark weird, but I didn't see it when I was scrubbing the sink, which seems impossible.

I straighten, moving my eyes back to the mirror. Beyond my reflection, in the open doorway behind me, stands a little girl, her deep burgundy hair flowing past her shoulders in long waves. A startled yip rips out of me, followed by a sharp inhale that drags frothing toothpaste into my lungs. I drop both brushes and spit, coughing and sputtering. I turn on the water and cup my hand under the faucet, swishing the rest of the toothpaste out of my mouth before using my dry hand to shut the faucet off, my wet one stretching to yank my towel off the floor. I race out of the bathroom, covering my mouth with the towel as I continue to cough.

"Hey!" I race through the hallway, looking for the child. "Where are you? It's okay, I won't hurt you. I just need to know who you are and how you got into my house." A splash of burgundy catches my eye, the tips of her long hair spraying out behind her as she disappears down the stairwell. I chase after her, pausing to glance into my room to be sure she wasn't in here stealing. Everything looks the same as it did when I woke up.

I run for the stairs, bounding down the steps two at a time. At the bottom, I look to the right, toward the front door. Nothing. I swivel left, deeper into the narrow corridor that leads to Mom's sitting room. I walk softly in that direction, peeking around the doorframe and searching the space. A door slams in the back of the house. I spin away from the sitting room and sprint in the direction of the slam. Mom hobbles out of her room at the end of the hall. "Watch out!" I yelp.

Her eyes fly wide, hand shooting up as if I'm about to strike her and she's trying to block the blow. I sweep my arms out and grab her, softening the collision and holding her upright as I come to a stop and calm my breathing "Sorry. I didn't mean to run into you, I'm just chasing that kid." I gently place my hand on her arm and lower her fingers back to her cane, moving myself away from her trembling body. "Did you see which way the kid went?"

Mom's lips flop open a few times, eyes squinting. "What kid?"

I shrug, shoving the hand still fisting the towel toward both the back of the house and the front. "I don't know who she is, just some little burgundy-headed kid who ran through here right before we collided. You didn't see her?"

Mom leans her weight onto her cane and looks around. "The only person I've seen is you, and I wish I didn't have to. When are you leaving, Valerie? I'm tired of you people barging in here like you're the one footing the bills around here."

I scrub the towel down my face, still feeling the dryness of toothpaste spatter all over it. "Unless this kid's name is Valerie, I have no idea who you're talking about, so help yourself to a seat in the kitchen and I'll be there to make your breakfast soon."

I shake off the disgust thickening Mom's voice as she professes she'd rather eat dirt than my cooking. As hard as it is to continually bite my tongue when she constantly berates me, the bruising on her arms from where I had to wrestle her back into the house last night is serving to keep my tongue locked up tight. At least tighter than it was with Crusty. I might have my own battle scars from Mom's temper tantrum, but I was still truly in rare form when talking to him. Maybe my mood was a premonition. I should have left at the first sign of not being able to keep my emotions in check. I almost slept with Luke, for goodness' sake.

I check the handle of the exterior door that leads onto a tiny stoop of a back porch that has more missing and broken boards than whole rotting pieces. It's locked, and I doubt even a kid brave enough to break into someone's house would dare traverse that porch. I peek out the window beside the door and don't see anyone outside. I spin around. This house is big. For all I know, this kid could be hiding in a cupboard.

I trek into the kitchen where Mom is rummaging around, pretending to look for food when what she's really doing is looking for the liquor she stored inside the cracker box she's holding. "You're fresh out." I smirk. "I'll grab you some more of those crackers while I'm out today, and all you'll find in the box will be actual crackers. So I hope you like them." She throws the empty box on the floor and scowls at me. I sigh. "Sit down. I'm going to make some biscuits and eggs. It won't take long, and maybe the smell will entice our little houseguest to show herself again."

~*10*~

S o far, Mom has demolished two biscuits and eaten a piece of ham. She refuses to touch the eggs, though. She claims not to like eggs, which I know for a fact is a lie. Eggs were the only thing she ever cooked for either of us when I was a kid. Breakfast, lunch, dinner...if she was cooking, it was eggs. Otherwise, it was condiment sandwiches and dry cereal because whenever Mom bothered to pick up groceries, it was eggs, bread, ketchup, and a bag of whatever cheap knock-off cereal she felt like. The ketchup went on the eggs, and she would sometimes serve them with a slice of bread. The cereal, according to her, was meant to be eaten with water. Every time she mixed that mush up for herself, it turned my stomach. My bowls of cereal were shoveled down dry.

"Mom, instead of complaining the entire time, how about you just eat the food you're given? I don't even need a thank you. All I want is for you to eat."

"Thank you?" She puffs, giving her hand a limp wave. "For what? You making messes in my kitchen that you're too lazy to clean up?" She flings the plate of eggs off the table. "No, you want me to thank you for you coming in here being such a bad cook we're both going to die of food poisoning."

I push my seat away from the table and get up. "I don't expect anything from you. Never have. Never will. And you can accuse me of anything you like, just so long as you keep putting food in your belly because my eggs aren't what's going to lead to your demise."

I tug a roll of paper towels from the counter and scrape the ruined eggs off the floor, piling the mess back onto the plate that's now donning a fresh chip along the edge. For as long as I've been alive and of an age to remember, Mom has gotten government assistance for nothing more than being a drunk who refuses to work. I never saw any of the money she was given each month, and that includes what was allotted for food. She traded all of it for booze and other little trinkets her twisted mind thought would be fun to have. The only full meal I ever got was at school. Or at Conner's when his parents would cook outside on their little grill. They'd invite me over for hotdogs or hamburgers, but I didn't start taking them up on the offer until after Conner asked me to be his girlfriend.

I pull myself out of my thoughts of the past and walk to the trashcan, dumping the plate and all inside. "Since our houseguest didn't join us for breakfast, I guess the kid doesn't like eggs either."

The legs of Mom's chair scrape over the linoleum as she attempts to slide it back so she can get up. "She's a smart girl, then. Unlike the meddling, no-good-for-nothin' brat I was saddled with."

I pull Mom's chair back and fit the handle of her cane into her palm. "You're ever-changing levels of vitriol are what I like most about you, and that's saying a lot because until today, I wasn't aware that I liked anything about you."

I walk Mom out of the kitchen and through the old Victorian halls. This place creaks and squeaks, but what I heard earlier was a slam. The little girl somehow managed to get out of the house. Probably the same way she managed to get inside. "You're sure you didn't see a kid run past your room right before you stepped into the hall?"

"I'm sure," Mom grumbles, muttering more insults under her breath.

I ignore the insults and keep her steady as I lead her into the mold room. "You didn't hear a door slam, either?"

She grunts, yanking her arm from my grip as she plops down into her chair, the noise and the sentiment clear. She wants me to stop speaking to her as much as she wants me to stop touching her. "The only thing I hear is the sound of your nagging voice whining in my ear. If your food doesn't kill me, having to listen to your mouth will."

"Hmm," I muse, crossing the room to flip on her DVD player. "We wouldn't want that, so I'll leave you in here to enjoy another exciting day of reruns."

I leave the room contemplating whether or not Mom let the little girl into the house and then hid her away just to mess with me. I wouldn't put a trick like that past her, but while the biscuits were baking, I searched everywhere I could think to look. Unless the girl is in the damp basement, which I highly doubt since the slide lock is still in place, the kid is long gone. Plus, Mom looks more the part of an evil witch, not a fairytale princess, so what kid would get close enough to be coerced by her?

I go outside and circle the house, looking for broken windows or other ways the kid could have gotten in without coming through a locked door. I stop at the back right corner to inspect a hole some kind of critter must have dug near the house's foundation. A car horn toots. I turn around and spot Luke pulling into the driveway. He parks and gets out of his cruiser, throwing a hand up in a wave. Before he can also shout a hello, I hurry to his location, glancing toward the house and hoping that Mom really is hard of hearing because I'd rather her not get curious as to who is outside blowing their horn. "What are you doing here?"

He leans on the hood of his vehicle, pressing his fingertips to the cut on his swollen lip. "I came to apologize for last night. I should have walked you out of the bar instead of letting Conner get to me."

I fold my arms over my chest. "I didn't need an escort, but yeah, you definitely shouldn't have let him get to you. Not only are you a cop whose reputation should matter, but I'm sure fistfighting your wife's boyfriend in a bar isn't going to look good in your divorce proceedings."

He leans his head back and sighs. "I'd rather not refer to him as Abbie's anything, but considering your history with him, I guess I should have mentioned that he's the reason I'm getting divorced." He clears his throat. "In part, at least. It took both of them, him and my wife, for the affair to happen. So the blame isn't only his. It's her fault too."

I don't respond. He pushes off his cruiser. "Mine, too. I don't really like to admit that I have any blame in the situation, but I guess I did something wrong to cause Abbie to stray." He takes a hesitant step toward me. "The wounds are still *really* fresh, so that's why I didn't get into the details with you. It's because I'm hurt, not because I'm trying to use you. I like you, Sierra. I always did. Every word I said to you last night was true. I was never brave enough to tell you how I felt when we were in school together. I tried, but then you and Conner started dating and I was either a better man than he is or a dang fool because I didn't think I could just tell you how I felt when you already had a boyfriend. So I kept my mouth shut, and now here we are."

I glance back at the house, making sure Mom isn't peeking out a window. My eyes float up to the elaborate hoods perched over the dirt-streaked windows. Like Conner and me, this place was once something. "Now here we are," I mutter in agreement.

Luke kicks a rock off to the side. "You don't have to like me back, obviously. I just needed to let you know what's going on inside my head and apologize for last night, including for how strong I came on. When I saw you, you had the same effect on me as you always did. I forgot about everything else. Conner and Abbie were the farthest things from my mind. I answered your questions as best as I could, but I was so hellbent on getting a second chance at seeing if we might have a shot at being more than friends that I didn't consider how you might feel about the two of them, or even what kind of feelings you might still have for Conner." His head dips. "I was selfish, and I'm sorry."

I study the fit of his uniform. I know from dancing with him last night that what lies beneath is more than desirable. I also know that unlike Conner, Luke is still the same person I remember. "I appreciate the apology. I don't think you necessarily had a responsibility to tell me any details about what happened with your wife. Conner's part in it would have been nice to know, but only so I wasn't blindsided with the information." I reach out and rub his arm. "I'm sure it's hard for you to discuss, so I owe you an apology too. I apologize for being a detective and prying into so many things last night. I'm not sorry I stormed out and left you in the bar, though. What's happening between you and Conner has nothing to do with me and I won't let you two drag me into the middle of it."

Luke steps closer, brushing his fingers against mine, his smile once again spreading across his face with the ease of melted butter. A truck rumbles by and he chuckles, nodding to Conner's slow-moving vehicle. "Believe me, Conner wouldn't have stormed across that bar last night unless it had everything to do with you, but I couldn't care less if Conner is jealous or not. As far as I'm concerned, he has my wife to keep him company."

I hold my breath until Conner's truck disappears from view, panic rising in my chest at the thought of him turning around and having another fistfight with Luke in the middle of Mom's driveway. I slip my hand from Luke's caress, assuming the only reason Conner isn't in jail right now is because Luke was off duty last night. "I'm not sure what kind of crisis Conner is having but trust me when I tell you he can barely stand the sight of me. As for us, I appreciate you being honest with me but I'm only in town to get my mom situated. I don't yet know what that even means. I might be in town a month, or I could be here a year or more. Whatever time frame this ends up being, I *will* be leaving at the end of it. Poca isn't my home anymore."

Luke grins. "I'm not asking you to marry me, mainly because I'm already married." I roll my eyes and he laughs, parroting a dialed-down version of my thoughts from last night. "I'm only asking for a chance to keep you company from time to time. Like today. Can I buy you lunch? A friendly meal where I mind my manners a little better than I did last night?"

I want to say no but his easy nature has me agreeing. I could use the company, if only for one lunch. "I'm going by the library again a little later. Want to meet me there whenever you're ready for lunch?"

His smile eats up his whole face. "I want to meet you wherever you are." He leans down and presses a kiss to my cheek. "Mmm, you smell like biscuits."

"Homemade," I respond.

His eyes widen. "Then I'd like to meet you in my kitchen."

I laugh. "Manage to keep me out of your fight with Conner and I'll see about making you a batch of biscuits that will melt in your mouth."

He presses a hand to his heart and gives me a wink. "You are speaking my language. I'll pick you up from the library around noon."

~ 11 ~

I thought libraries were the places to go when you needed answers but today is proving to be another unfruitful day. There are plenty of old articles about the school fire but there's nothing in them that even hints at the prospect of the fire having been set intentionally. Surely the blaze would have been thoroughly investigated. Maybe B only took credit for something that happened on a night when he, or she, was upset.

I lean in to read another article, finger absently tracing over the sticker of the glittery letter K on the old-style mouse I have to use to navigate the equally old desktop computer. "Boo!" Luke whisper-shouts in my ear, grin growing wide as he slides into the seat next to mine. "You're not jumpy, that's good. But you still smell like biscuits."

"Better than smelling like Talico Bar," I grumble, dropping the tone and returning his smile. "Before you break all of the library's quiet rules trying to scare unsuspecting women, let me give you something to be noisy about." I reach into my oversized bag and pull out the container of biscuits I brought for him. "I managed to save you a few of this morning's haul. It wasn't easy, Mom is eating them by the dozen. All while complaining about what a terrible cook I am."

He shakes his head and takes a playful whiff of the plastic. "I don't even need to eat one to know her opinion is dead wrong. You smell too good for these not to be the best biscuits that have ever melted in my mouth." He winks and rests the container on his knee, the twinkle fading from his eyes. "How's your mom doing? I should have made more of a point to check in on her but after the way she acted the year you disappeared, I just never bothered going back over there."

My heart aches for him. I'm sure part of the reason he didn't want to go there is because of what his stepdad put him through in that house. "Mom wouldn't have talked to you even if you did try to check on her. Not unless you had alcohol on you."

He leans back in his chair and opens the container, snagging a biscuit and taking an oversized bite. I look over the top of the computer monitor, checking to see if Jan is watching. "I'm pretty sure you're not supposed to have food or drink in here."

He taps his uniform. "You'd be surprised what I can get away with when I'm wearing this. And I'm telling you right now, your mom is dead wrong."

He finishes off his biscuit in two more bites, licking his fingers with a devilish grin on his face. "Please tell me I'm invited to your place for breakfast tomorrow."

I push my seat back and reach for the yearbooks stacked beside me. "If you don't get me kicked out of the library, we'll see about breakfast."

Luke swipes the book off the top of the pile. It's from our junior year of high school. "What are you doing with these? Looking up old classmates?"

I hesitate. I'm still uneasy about mentioning the diary but if there really is an arsonist in town, the police should know about it. I motion to the article on the computer screen. "Do you remember the fire at the high school the summer before senior year?"

He glances at the news article about the fire. "Everyone remembers that. Why? Do you have a guilty conscience? Because another thing I get when I'm in uniform is people randomly confessing to all the minor crimes they've committed. Running traffic lights and walking out of a store with a can of soda pop they forgot to pay for." He scoots closer to me. "The hard criminals usually make me work a little more earnestly to get a confession out of them, and they never bribe me with biscuits."

I swat his arm. "I'm being serious. I want to know about the fire. Was anyone ever charged with setting it?"

He glances between me and the computer screen again. "No, Detective, but now you have me seriously considering why this is so important to you." He sets the yearbook and the biscuits aside, staring at me with what I assume is his *cop* look. "What do you know?"

I swallow. "Nothing. I just... Well, the cheerleaders were blamed for the fire but I never heard what exactly caused it. Not officially anyway. I, um, heard that one of the cheerleaders was fooling around with someone else's boyfriend and that the fire was retaliation. Could something like that be true?"

He studies me. "Where did you hear this?"

I look away and clasp my hands together, cringing with every lying word out of my mouth. I should just hand the diary over to him but for some reason, I don't want to. "I honestly can't remember. I'd forgotten about the whole thing until I was back here." I turn in my seat and face him. "Do you think Brian could have started the fire?"

Luke's arms fold over his chest. "Brian wasn't around that summer. He got to the point that he needed more than what those online classes could offer so the state provided some sort of assisted living. He and his mom moved before the end of the previous school year." Luke's head tilts. "Where is all of this coming from? If you know—"

A boom rattles the windows, like a bomb just exploded nearby. Luke jumps out of his seat and starts rattling words and numbers into the radio attached to his shoulder. More words and numbers spill back to him from the device. I grab the biscuits and follow him to the front of the library. He opens the door, sadness crawling through his features. "Raincheck on lunch?"

I nod, pressing the container into his hand. "Of course. Go. If I can help in some way, let me know."

He tucks the biscuits under his arm and leans down to press one of his soft kisses to my cheek. "Just stay here for a while. Emergency crews are en route and I don't know exactly what's going on yet. I'll text you when it's all clear."

I watch him run to his cruiser, standing in the doorway until his lights are on, sirens blaring, and he tears out of the parking lot. A tingling sensation itches at the back of my head. I rub at it, my palms sweating. Something isn't right. I don't feel good. I press a hand to my stomach and turn around, maybe I really did give myself food poisoning.

Jan is behind me. Her eyes dip to the hand on my stomach. "Are you okay?"

I clear my throat, my breath growing shallow. "I think so, just a little shaken up to see Luke run out of here like that. Do you think something blew up at one of the chemical plants across the river?"

Her lips turn up in a forced smile, a miserable attempt at being reassuring. "Things like that do happen from time to time. I wouldn't worry about Luke, though."

I give her what I'm sure is an equally fake smile and turn back toward my table. She reaches a hand out and presses it against my arm. "Don't take this the wrong way because I know you just got back into town and all, and that Luke sure is a charmer, but he's married, honey. And his wife is pregnant. They might be having a spat but when that baby of his comes, that child will do wonders when it comes to mending their relationship."

Guilt rides up my spine and my cheeks burn. Once again, Luke left out important details about his separation. "Thanks, Jan. Luke is only an old friend, and that's how things will stay."

~*12*~

Jan's words hit their mark, digging into my chest until my trip back to Mom's house is one fully hidden somewhere in the black hole of my memory. Even now, as I sit alone on my bed, I'm struggling to focus on anything other than the many reasons I've always felt like an outsider in Poca. Growing up here wasn't fun or exciting. I hated every part of the life I was born to. The sad, painful, and humiliating existence that came with having a mother whose love for the bottle far outweighed any touch of sentiment she had for her child.

If Mom had ever apologized for the words she assaulted me with, or expressed even a tiny bit of regret over her actions, I might have tolerated being here enough that I would have stayed in Poca. Maybe I would have been able to help her in some small way so that her health wouldn't be in the state of deterioration it is now. I doubt Conner and I would have stayed together, but I also doubt he'd violently hate me if he'd been the one to end things. He can blame Mom for that blow to his ego, though, because she's the one who never showed me an ounce of care. She didn't uplift or encourage. There were no little moments of clarity, no remorse for humiliating me by being passed out on the lawn where all the kids could see her when the school bus arrived. I took the humiliation for as long as I could, never able to escape it. All I could do was escape her.

I flip open another one of the yearbooks I had enough conscious thought to check out from the library. This one is from my sophomore year, and my eyes immediately land on Taylor Ray, her smiling face peeking overtop red and gray pom-poms. Her mom was loud, blunt, and always sipping from a thermos everyone knew held adult-beverage contents. Only Taylor's mom wasn't a sloppy and disheveled drunk like mine. Taylor's mom was clean, well dressed, and planned all of the cheer team's fundraisers. She was involved in Taylor's life and those of her friends. She was a functioning alcoholic instead of an alcoholic whose only function was to drink.

I lean against the wooden slats of my headboard and flip through the pages, stopping on Conner's class picture. This was the year things really heated up between us. There wasn't a teenage hormone we left unquenched. The boy next door dating the girl next door. Classic. Cliché. And yet neither of those things. Because while Conner's family lived in the trailer park alongside me, what happened inside their walls was so incredibly different from anything I ever experienced inside my own. None of us were blessed with money, but his parents were happy and they selflessly cared for him and his two older brothers, doing everything within their power to make sure their boys always had what they needed.

Tires crunch over Mom's gravel driveway, the soft rumble of a truck engine one that makes my stomach tighten into a knot. I slide the book off my lap and jump out of bed, crossing the room and pulling the edge of the threadbare curtain back to find Conner's truck coming to a stop beside my car. Great. If touching his photograph is the way to summon him, I'll never again even look at a picture of Conner Ferguson.

I drop the curtain and dart out of the room, jogging down the stairs. I managed to snap out of my trance earlier just in time to make Mom's dinner. She's been in bed for the past half hour and the last thing I need is her waking up because Conner is pounding on the door. He *will* pound, too, because I doubt this new adult version of him has the capacity to politely knock.

I fling the front door open just as his balled fist is rising to beat on the wood. He lowers his hand. I push him away from the door and step out onto the porch, closing the house up behind me and instantly being overwhelmed by the strong smell of smoke clinging to the air around him. "What do you want, Conner? I'm already home, so I still don't need a ride from you."

His eyes narrow. His mouth opens but a flash of burgundy hair catches the corner of my eye. I turn toward it, running across the porch, down the steps, and away from him. "Hey!" We both yell. Conner at me, and me at the little girl who just ducked into the row of shoulder-high shrubs that line the driveway and beyond, forming a border all the way down the side of the house.

I race around his truck and to the mouth of the shrubs where the kid disappeared. "Come out of there!" I yell into the bushes.

Conner comes up behind me, pressing close and leaning around me to shake the foliage. "There's nothing in there."

I grab a branch farther down and shake. "Yes, there is. This kid already broke into the house once and she must have been trying to get in again."

Conner snakes an arm around my waist and leans his long body around the bushes, scanning the other side. "These shrubs aren't thick enough to hide a cat, let alone a kid, and we need to talk, so quit whatever game you're trying to play. I'm not here because I can't keep myself away from you, Sierra."

I let go of the leafy branch in my hand and look down the long row that separates this lot from the next, tapping the fingers he has plastered against my stomach. "Could've fooled me, Conner." And to the kid, I yell, "Stay out of my house! If you don't, I'm going to find you!"

Conner anchors me against him, tipping my feet off the ground and forcing me back to the house. "I don't know what's wrong with you, Sierra, but I do know I haven't looked for you *once* and I wouldn't be talking to you now if you didn't come back here."

I try prying his arm off me but he only tightens his grip. "There are a lot of things wrong with me, and today *two* big problems are a kid who keeps breaking into my house and *you* assaulting me."

He carries me up the steps and to the front door. "Your problem is having an ego that can't stand not getting its way."

I snort, flinging my body sideways in a failed attempt to keep him from opening the front door. He shoves it open against my will and muscles me inside, slamming it shut behind him. "Stop," I growl. "I just got my mom to bed and I swear if you wake her up..."

He walks forward, mouth lowering to my ear as he hauls me up the steps. "You swear what? What are you going to do to me if I don't let you have your way?"

I kick my heel into his shin, teeth bared. "You're the one with an ego problem, not me. Put. Me. Down."

He tops the stairs with my struggling body and maneuvers down the hall to my bedroom. I'm not impressed with his little show of strength. He was the athletic beast of his little *cool-kids* clique, while I was only his inconvenient plus-one. I'm equally unimpressed that he remembers where my old bedroom is. I didn't live in this house very long and he didn't drop by much, but when he did, this rickety old bed is where we spent our time. Since he didn't even bother to wonder where I was, the least he can do is remember where I satisfied his every desire.

I kick his leg again and he tosses me onto the bed. I scramble to my knees, ready to fight, but he's turned away from me and is storming back across the room. He grips the edge of my door, his motion wanting to slam it or break it, but instead, he musters the effort to shut it gently. I spring off the bed and he turns back toward me. I charge in his direction, bent on sending him right back out that door. He meets me in the center of the room, his big hands shooting out and clamping around my wrists. "Stop," I grind out, still sensitive to any noise that will wake Mom up.

He gives me a snapping jerk, forcing my eyes to stare into his. There's fear in the icy depths, mixing and weaving with a turmoil that douses my rage. "What is it?" My voice rattles. I try to reach for him but he pins my arms to my sides. "Conner, what's wrong? What happened?"

His nostrils flare. "You don't know?"

I struggle against his grip. "All I know is that you're scaring me. And hurting me."

His fingers tighten and my toes curl under as he hauls me closer to him. "Rusty's trailer blew up, and the inferno caused by the explosion managed to take half of Talico Bar to ash with it. *That's* pain, Sierra. A man burning alive inside his own home is what *hurts*."

My knees go weak. "Burned alive..."

Conner flicks his wrists, crashing my chest against him while his arms stretch around me, keeping me upright. "I'm not the only one who knows you had words with Rusty last night, and now he's dead. So instead of yelling at little kids and worrying about your mom waking up, you tell me where you've been since you drove away from me like a woman looking for the kind of trouble she's getting ready to find herself in."

~13~

I'm a rag doll in Conner's arms. Shock has my limbs as cooperative as spaghetti. He hauls me to the bed and plops me down. I roll onto my side and grip the edge, leaning my head over and sucking in air. "That boom earlier..." I struggle to form words, the news coupled with his accusation crippling my ability to breathe. "It was Crusty's trailer?"

"Grow up, Sierra!" Conner shouts. "The man is dead. It was funny to call him Crusty when you were a kid but you're not a freaking kid anymore. Rusty might not have been a good person but he was a human being. He has a family!"

My throat constricts. "Crusty was married?"

Conner paces away from me. "You're freaking unbelievable. You know that?" His footsteps pound past the bed and back across the room. "Is that why you did it? Rusty wasn't married so you thought you'd blow him up and his sister and her kids wouldn't care?"

I let go of the bed and shove myself upright, leaning my weight against the frame. "No, Conner, I didn't think that because I didn't kill him. I don't even know how a person could possibly make a double-wide blow up."

He walks back toward me. Slowly. "By rigging his propane tank, Sierra. That was the explosion the whole town heard. But you already knew that, didn't you?"

I bite back the ball of emotion pushing its way up my throat. "No, I didn't know what the explosion was until you just told me. And for your information, I've never even used a propane tank before. I don't know the first thing about them, so find someone else to accuse of murder because it was *not* me."

His hands clench into fists at his sides, fingers stretching back open again and repeating the process, as if he's itching to do something with those hands. He stops in front of me, his voice even and steady. "After you drove away pouting and mad because you didn't like not getting your way, I went back into the bar. Rusty told me you were in there giving him a hard way to go. After the fight that broke out, he told *a lot* of people about you, letting them know you were only in his bar to cause trouble for him."

I spring up like a lightning bolt, staring him in the eye even though tears are threatening mine. "*You* caused that fight, not me. I went into Talico Bar to have a civil conversation with *Crusty* Rusty but he showed no sign of being a reasonable human. Ask Luke. He was there for part of that exchange, and unlike you and Rusty, Luke is actually a decent person to have a conversation with. Which is what I was doing with him until *you* came along acting like a jealous lover." I step into him. "Don't worry, I know it wasn't me you were jealous of. It was Luke's wife. I hear she's having his baby and wants to reconcile with him. That must really bruise your pouty, fragile, mad-because-you're-not-getting-to-eat-your-cake-and-have-it-too ego. *You* are the one used to getting their way, not me."

Conner latches onto my arms just below my shoulders. "I interrupted your dance because everything I told you about Luke is true. He's using you as a prop, someone whose biscuits he can parade around town and throw in the face of his wife. Just like that scumbag daddy of his used to do to his own wife, coming home smelling like perfume and telling her she should find out what kind of scent it is so she could wear a perfume that would let him close his eyes and relive whatever sick things his badge coerced some young female into doing with him."

I stop struggling and fix my eyes on his. "Are you saying Luke isn't separated? That he's cheating on his wife and abusing her and others? That's what drove her into your arms?"

Conner lets go of me. "I'm telling you that Luke was at that inferno today making time to brag about your biscuits, and not only for my benefit. As you pointed out, he heard you having words with Rusty. Luke brought that little fact up right in front of me, telling one of the other officers that you were worked up over the situation with Rusty, so he bought you a beer to calm you down." Conner's eyes blaze. "In return, he says you made him breakfast."

The oxygen in the room is once again hard to come by. I step backward and slowly lower myself to the bed. Conner didn't fully answer my questions but he's said enough. "Luke is implying we spent the night together?"

Conner's brow cocks. "Did you?"

I glare at him. "No. Which is why you saw him here in his uniform this morning. Unlike you, he had the good sense to come and apologize to me."

Conner runs both of his hands up his face and through his hair, his own breath leaving his chest in a long sigh. "Good. I think."

"You think?" I gape at him. "What is going on? You're slinging accusations, none of which make any sense, by the way, and you think it *might* be good that I didn't sleep with a man you say is a mirror image of Gerald Putnam?"

Conner studies the cracked ceiling. "I'm tired, Sierra. I haven't slept since you got back here and now…" He looks at me. "Luke was definitely insinuating he slept with you, and he dragged your name into the conversation by first implying you had motive to attack Rusty. Did you really tell Rusty you were going to burn down his walls?"

Memories of the sharp tongue I wielded that night cut into my thoughts. I fist the bedcover. "I was mad, and I might have said something like that, but I was speaking figuratively." Conner shakes his head at me. I shake mine right back at him. "Clearly, you think I blew a man up, but Luke does too? He's blaming me for the explosion?"

Conner's stare goes distant. "I don't see any other reason for him to put you in the context that he did today unless he's trying to get you on a suspect list while giving himself a reason to have been with you that doesn't implicate him as being complicit." He focuses back on me. "Answer me honestly. Did you rig the explosion? Did you somehow drag Luke into it so now he's trying to save his own skin?"

"No," I bark. "How can you even think I would do something like that?"

He snorts. "Why don't you tell me? Because the last time I saw you, you weren't the girl I grew up fifty feet away from."

I think back to the night I left Poca. It's all such a blur, snippets of walking down dimly lit streets alone, crying, emotion scratching out of me and leaving my heart on the blacktop. I look down at the floor. "I just...snapped. I had to get away. But you were all I ever had, Conner. And not only when I was in Poca. After I left, I spent years missing you. Mourning you. Losing you is a pain I don't know if I'll ever get over." I look up at him. "I've learned to live with it, though. I'm sorry you haven't, but how dare you barge in here, manhandle me, and throw my past in my face like you have any idea what I've been through. I was an emotionally distraught seventeen-year-old kid the last time you saw me, and I was a distraught and destitute adult until a few years ago. Now I have myself together and you do *not* get to come in here and tear me down."

He kneels in front of me and lifts his hand to my face. I flinch away. He lowers his hand to my knee. "I know you didn't leave here and go on to live some glamorous life. How could you have?" He squeezes my knee. "A part of me hoped you did, and the other part resented you for even being outside the borders of Poca."

"I guess we know which side won." I sniff.

He stretches back to his full height and paces away from me, circling the room. "Why couldn't you just trust me, Sierra? All you had to do was trust me enough to talk to me about what was going on in that head of yours. I would have helped you."

Tears spill onto my cheeks because I know it's true. I could have talked to Conner about anything back then, I just didn't want to. I hated being the one with problems. It was bad enough that most of his friends barely acknowledged me. A few of the girls even asked him out right in front of me.

Conner stops beside the bed and reaches down to wipe my tears. "Hey, I'm sor... What is this?" He reaches behind me and tugs the open yearbook off the bed.

I swipe at the tears racing down my cheeks and grab another book. His senior year. Not mine, since I was barely here for it. Against my better judgment, I flip to where the class pictures are and look for me. There's nothing. Not even a notation that I'm *not pictured*. "I picked these up at the library today. Looks like everyone decided to take a cue from my mother and not give a damn about me."

He throws the book back onto the bed. "People cared about you, you just didn't like yourself enough to see it."

I flip to the page his picture is on. Handsome, as always, but not smiling the way he usually did for school photos. Two rows above his picture is an empty black square with a glittery heart in the middle of it. Underneath the missing photograph is a name. Kaity Bell Edwards. She was part of Conner and Luke's friend group. A perky little blonde who was always smiling. One of those goody-goody types that went out of her way to pay everyone a compliment, as if she was trying to win a congeniality award. She was also a cheerleader. I tap her black square, pointing out to Conner how unlike me, the school bothered to not only list Kaity's name but they held an entire spot for her. "Thank you for the therapy session. You can go now."

He rips the book from my hands. "Are you serious right now?"

I get off the bed and cross the floor, opening the door and holding it for him. At least all the Ks plastered around town have a meaning now. I don't know what happened to Kaity, but two girls aren't in that yearbook and only one of them is a person people deem worthy of remembering. "Yeah, I am. I had *nothing* to do with Rusty's death, the explosion, or anything else that happened anywhere in Poca today. If you're here because you're worried I'm going to mess up your affair with Luke's wife, don't be. I wouldn't dream of getting in the middle of the three of you. I'm not in Poca to rekindle old flames or even old friendships. I'm here because of the stupid obligation I feel to take care of the woman who gave birth to my miserable existence."

A sob breaks from my throat but I hold my head high. Conner tosses the book onto the bed and crosses the room, stopping in front of me. He runs a rough thumb under my eye, the muscles in his arm tightening as he does. "I barely got through senior year because of you. I almost flunked out. I didn't play in a single football game and I got kicked off the basketball team. So don't you worry, I'm not going to let you come back here and get in the middle of anything. You're not going to ruin what little life I've been able to build for myself after the messed-up seventeen-year-old girl I loved with every breath I took ripped out my heart and destroyed any chance of me ever living a happy life."

The lump in my throat cuts off my words. I reach up to wipe the tear that's running down his cheek but he smacks my hand away and ducks out of the room. His pounding footsteps echo back from the stairwell. The front door slams, rattling the walls of this old house. "Go away!" Mom yells out. I shut my bedroom door. Softly. With any luck, she'll think it was me leaving and she'll go back to sleep. But luck doesn't favor me, so if she doesn't go back to sleep, she can keep yelling. I've done my duty for Mom today. I can't deal with anything more.

I walk back to the bed. I've never seen Conner cry before and knowing I'm the reason he's shedding tears right now is devastating. He was such a good person before and now I *know* I'm responsible for the change in his personality. I destroyed all of the happiness that lived inside him. The same way Mom destroyed mine.

~14~

Sleep didn't come easily last night. Every time I closed my eyes, I saw Conner standing in front of me, unshed tears clinging to his lashes. Then came the weight of his accusation, my chest aching from Conner coming here believing I was involved in Rusty's death. I'd gasp for air, the words Conner spoke echoing through my mind the way his footsteps echoed off the stairs. Whenever I calmed down enough, I'd drift back off to sleep thinking of how in the two and a half years we officially dated, Conner never once said he loved me.

I never said those words to him either, so maybe he's right and I didn't know he cared about me as much as I loved him because I was too scared to believe it could be true. If I asked and he didn't love me back, I would have been devastated. So I pretended our relationship was fine the way it was, Conner having all the perks that a girlfriend could bring to a boy's life while also having the complete freedom of a boy without a girlfriend. I usually didn't even go to parties with him. The invites were only for him, and on the occasions when I'd give in and go with him, I spent the whole night knowing I didn't belong.

Conner did always try his best to make me feel wanted in those situations, but I didn't *want* him to have to spend his time worrying about whether or not I was having a good time. It was better to just let him go alone. He did, and every time I wondered if that would be the night he hooked up with someone else. I waited for him to kick me to the curb but after every party, he came to me. Maybe that's the real reason he lost his way when I left Poca. The convenience of dating someone like me couldn't be replaced by anyone else in town. If Conner really loved me, he wouldn't have wanted to go to places where I wasn't welcome.

I wipe the sleep from my eyes and pull the stack of yearbooks off my vintage mahogany nightstand. The old piece of furniture would probably be worth something if it wasn't chipped on two corners and scratched up like a cat preferred filing its nails with wood instead of carpet.

I flip through the pages of Conner's senior yearbook aiming straight for the back where group photos of the sports teams are located, including the cheerleaders. Instead of worrying about Conner's feelings for me, I need to scan the faces of the cheerleaders because if B's diary *is* real, then in some twisted way, one of these girls was the target of the school fire, and the arsonist got away with their deed. Then, a day after I go into Talico Bar asking about the former tenants of Mom's house, the one person who has that information is burned alive. Coincidence? Maybe. If it isn't, I need to know which of these cheerleaders ticked off a fire starter.

I flip to a group photo where the girls are all wearing black jumpsuits instead of their cheer uniforms. Their blonde hair and heavy makeup stick out atop the solid black clothing. There was a joke in town that in order to be a cheerleader in Poca, the only qualification was having blonde hair and a tube of red lipstick. That applied to everyone but me. Throughout the years, I was never invited to join the team. In grade school, I went to tryouts and was ignored by every child and adult in the gymnasium. I sat on the edge of the bleachers until the very end, the cheerleading coach making obvious attempts not to acknowledge me. When she thanked everyone for coming and people started leaving, I got up and did backflips all the way across the floor, the last one landing me in front of the emergency exit. I didn't bother to scan the faces of the people in the room before I left. I saw what the other kids did and I knew I was a better tumbler than all of them. It was enough that they knew it, too.

I'd worked hard to teach myself how to do backflips in the spot of grass between my trailer and Conner's. That's when I first became friends with the boy next door. When he wasn't off with the other kids, he'd sit on the edge of his porch and egg me on. He's the one who put it my head to go to that tryout, and afterward he'd still encourage me but I never again attempted to try out for the squad. I couldn't afford to be on the team anyway. All of the girls wore a particular brand of shoe and each team member was responsible for buying their own uniforms. So I acted as if being a cheerleader was stupid because back then, I couldn't even afford a tube of the cheap red lipstick they wore. All of my clothes came from a local charity, even my undergarments. At first, I accepted it as just my way of life. Then one of the girls in school made fun of me for wearing that pink dress Luke remembered. It was her hand-me-down from the previous year. I stopped going to school dances after that.

I wonder if Conner went to any dances after I left. He didn't while we were officially dating but I'm sure he went to his senior prom. Probably with one of these girls. I lean closer to the picture in front of me. It's odd because none of the cheerleaders are smiling. In their all-black attire, they're stoic as they hold up banner-style signs. The one in the back row reads *Justice for Kaity*. The middle row says *Find Kaity*. The one in the front, pulled tight between the girls who are kneeling, reads *We love you, Kaity*. On the cheek of each individual cheerleader is a glitter-crusted K, just like the ones sprinkled all over town.

I put the yearbook down and grab the one from my junior year, flipping to where Kaity's smiling face is on the same page as Conner's. Both of them, and all of the other kids around them, look so young and innocent. A stark contrast to the cheerleaders' group photo in the senior yearbook, with Kaity's missing picture and Conner's frowning face.

I slide the book away and reach for B's diary, sitting up and pulling it onto my lap. Familiar pieces clink together in my mind as I flip it open to the next entry.

July 5, 2012

Last night was crazy. In a watch-out-or-the-zombie-is-going-to-eat-your-face kind of way. I hardly ever get to go out, show my true self, and have the kind of fun I had with my boyfriend last night. He was reluctant to celebrate Independence Day with the bang I had in mind until I fed him a delicious little square of acid. After he devoured that, and me, he was an animal. Not a street sign or car window in Poca was safe. Neither was the cheer-squad drama queen. She didn't learn her lesson in the fire so I gave her another one. We stole her car and drove it into the river, watching it sink until the headlights blinked out.

I gasp. I remember a silver Volvo going missing. It was never found and belonged to Kaity Bell Edwards. A pain begins to throb behind my right eye. I rub at my temple and read the rest of the entry.

My sisters said I shouldn't have urged my boyfriend to do things he would never do if he wasn't on acid, but I say you never really know yourself until you tear down the walls of your inhibition.

Isn't that right, Snooper? I bet you feel a little anxious when it's dark. You should.

Someone's always there...

B.

I drop the diary and reach for a pen, my shaking hands dropping the blue ballpoint onto the folds of my blanket. Time slows to a crawl as I pick it back up. The diary's author just issued a threat to whoever is reading their words. Considering the timing of Rusty's brutal death, I don't think the threat remained in 2012. I need to make a list of every person I know whose name starts with B. It doesn't matter if they've lived in this house or not because I'm no longer sure B did live here. Maybe the boyfriend lived here. Or maybe a burgundy-haired little girl stole the diary from someone and deposited it in this rickety old house for safekeeping. That would explain why the book wasn't ruined. It hasn't been here for eleven years. And the girl snuck back inside these walls to either retrieve the book or to see if I found it.

I glance at the black fabric covering the diary, a shiver crawling up my spine at the thought of B ordering the little messenger girl to leave the book here for me to find. Why— "Sierra!" A croaking voice scratches over my ears, sending my bones jumping and my head slamming into the hard wood of the headboard. A yelp escapes my lips just as Mom yells again. "Sierra! Get down here, tramp!"

She's screaming with the full force of everything she's got in her lungs, which isn't much. I rub what's going to be a big sore lump in about an hour and decide it's a win that Mom at least made me jump out of my skin while using my actual name. For the most part. The smell of burned toast hits my nostrils and I lean over to the nightstand, checking the time on my barely used phone. "Dang it." I throw the covers back and rush out of the room. "Coming! Sorry, I overslept," I offer, not that she'll accept the apology or even care that I barely slept last night. Still, I hurry into the bathroom and grab the mouthwash, gargling and spitting before splashing water on my face. This will have to do for now. If she's burning toast and yelling for me to come downstairs, there's a chance the meal schedule I'm trying to get her on is taking root.

I race to the stairs, bounding down them two at a time, my tattered shirt letting a chill sink into my bones. I've slept in this same shirt nearly every night since I left Poca. It's to the point of being so threadbare that the pieces without holes and rips are practically see-through. I dart through the narrow hallway and turn right, skidding to a halt when I see Conner at the kitchen sink, the toaster upturned as he shakes the blackened bread out of it. "I told him it was broken," Mom mutters from her seat at the table.

He scowls at her. "And I told your mom that if we couldn't figure out how to make toast on our own, then we didn't deserve to eat." His eyes move away from her and stop cold as they land on me. He scans the ratty, ripped-up t-shirt sitting atop my too-short cotton shorts. His gaze moves slowly down my body, taking in my bare legs. He licks his lips and glues his eyes to mine. "Besides, I thought we were having biscuits this morning."

I shove my feet into motion, detaching them from the patch of floor they're trying to glue themselves to. I march to the sink, praying this t-shirt is too worn and faded for Conner to realize it's his. I yank the toaster out of his hands. "There are plenty of restaurants where you can go eat as many biscuits as you like, and Mom is right, this toaster is broken. You have to manually pop the toast up or else it burns. Like this." I pull the blackened bread from the sink and wave it in front of his face.

"Wasn't broken until you got here," Mom growls, low and almost to herself.

I slide the toaster back onto the counter. "Yes, it was broken, but you were on a liquid diet before I got here so you didn't know that you couldn't make a piece of toast without nearly catching the house on fire."

Conner turns and leans against the counter. "This place is more of a dump on the inside than it is on the exterior, so burning it down isn't a bad idea. Too bad it doesn't have a propane tank out back."

I glare at him. I'm not going to engage Conner with Mom in the room. She doesn't need to know anything about my personal life or what the people in it are accusing me of. I also haven't yet told her that Rusty is dead. She should hear it from me, not anyone else. "Maybe there's a propane tank at your house. You should go home and check." I shove past Conner and yank a mixing bowl out of the cabinet behind him. "I'm buying you a new toaster this week, Mom. It's already on my list of things you need."

She lifts her cane, doing her best to shake it at me but barely getting it off the floor. "About time. If you're going to freeload, you might as well do something useful. I'm not running a boarding house for moochers."

Conner opens his mouth but I slam a bag of flour on the counter beside him, giving him a look that I hope he interprets correctly. He knows what my mom is like, and therefore he knows that engaging her will only make things worse. He sighs and crosses his muscled arms over his chest.

Satisfied that he's going to bite his tongue, I drag a whisk from the water pitcher I put on the counter to hold the new kitchen utensils I picked up. I should have brought my stuff from Dallas but I didn't want to bring anything with me that made it feel like I was here to stay.

Conner watches me take eggs from the refrigerator. I slide them next to the flour and lean into his personal space, keeping my voice low. "Why are you here?"

He nods to the ingredients piling up beside him. "I need some of that flaky, melt-in-your-mouth dough I had to hear so much about yesterday."

I pull back into my own space, still too close to him, and break the eggs into the bowl while glaring at him. "You should have asked Luke to share then. Or does he not share his food? Only his wife?" His eyes narrow. I smile. "That's right, he didn't share his wife either. You just helped yourself."

Conner pushes off the counter and moves into place behind me, his chest to my back and his muscled arms circling to rest on the counter beside my bowl, pinning me in place. He lowers his mouth to my ear, his deep voice smooth and his hot breath feathering over my neck. "I didn't think you wanted to do this in front of your mom, but I'm game if you are." He runs his nose along my ear. "I don't need anything that belongs to Luke. I have my own, and I'll be helping myself to everything that's *mine*."

A loud knock resounds through the house. Conner stiffens. So do I. It's one thing for Conner to see me half naked but wholly another for a perfect stranger. Conner's hands lift from the counter as another loud knock sounds, this one beating five times instead of three. "I've got it. You just keep working on my breakfast, long legs."

~*15*~

There's no way I'm letting Conner answer the door. "Stop it." I swat his hands. He's shuffling down the hall with me, picking and pulling at my shirt and fitting his fingers through the holes.

He caresses the skin along my side, a cocky grin on his face like we're playing a sweet little game the way lovers do. "I can't believe you kept my shirt. I still remember the day I slipped it over your head to cover your beautiful body before my brother walked in on us."

I shove him away from me, pinning him with a glare that dares him to do or say anything else. "You will *not* answer a door at my house."

The banging on the door continues and the person wanting entry calls my name through the wood. "Sierra?"

My heart drops. Conner narrows his eyes at the wood separating him from Luke. "This isn't your house, it's Wanda's, and he isn't welcome here." Conner pulls my hand into his. "Get rid of him, or I'll do it for you."

I try to tug my hand free, his words and the tingling sensation on my side from his hands being on me deflating all the meaning from the motion. Which he knows, because he's drawing his mouth back into that cocky grin I wish I wanted to slap off his face rather than kiss. He traces my exposed shoulder with his eyes, running them all the way down to the hand he's holding. He turns my arm over and then reaches for the other, taking note of the still healing gouges Mom left on me. His eyes flash back to mine and I yank out of his grip. "You know what she's like so stop acting surprised." I point at the floor. "Stay."

He takes an intentional step forward and then leans against the wall, sweeping an arm forward as if giving me permission to answer my own door. I flip him off and traverse the remaining few feet to the once stately entrance, slipping out onto the porch and shutting the door behind me. There's no hiding the fact that Conner's here. His truck is in the driveway and Luke knows the vehicle well, as evidenced by the thick layer of betrayal in his eyes. I pretend I'm not practically in my birthday suit and lean against the closed front door, staring down at the porch in hopes of calming my flustered nerves. Conner has my heart racing for way too many reasons.

I inhale deeply and force myself to meet Luke's stare. There's a chance this isn't a social visit. If what Conner told me last night is true, there's one theory he didn't explore when it comes to Luke dragging my name into the conversation surrounding Rusty. Luke could have helped B rig Rusty's place to blow, and then went about his day spreading misinformation to point the investigation far away from him and his lover. I swallow. "I haven't checked my phone so I don't know if you texted last night, but I heard about Rusty's place. Are you okay? I mean, were any of the first responders hurt?"

Luke keeps his gaze level. "No, we're all fine. Thanks for asking."

I give him a casual nod, pretending tension isn't mounting all around us. He drops his eyes to my clothes. "Did a mouse get into your closet? Or a swarm of moths? Because you're missing quite a bit of thread in that shirt."

I run my hand over my exposed side. "This is just an old shirt that I sleep in. I haven't been out of bed long enough to shower and change."

His head tilts. "Is that because you had a late night?"

My heart jumps, my pulse picking up until the blood rushing through my ears is deafening. He's too standoffish for this to be a social call. He's here to interrogate me. I glance at his cruiser and then back at him. The door falls out from behind me and I keel backward, right into Conner's arms. "There you are, honey." He gives me a squeeze. "Everything okay out here? Our breakfast is getting cold."

I smack his hands away from me and lift off his chest. "Everything out here is just fine, so feel free to leave because I'm not eating your burned toast."

He chuckles, speaking words to let Luke know he's been listening at the door behind me the whole time. "After the late night we had, you're going to need to eat something, and soon. You can't be tired *and* hungry while sitting in the doctor's office all day, so hurry up and get rid of this magazine salesman. Mom's appointment is in a few hours."

"Really?" I challenge. He knows what he's doing by not only calling Luke a dismissive name, but also by referring to Wanda as if we're a couple and she's as endeared to him as I am.

He grins. "Really."

I turn away from him and grip Luke's arm. Maybe I should beg him to arrest me, just to get me away from Conner. I pull Luke from the porch and away from the glare-off he's trying to wage with Conner. I'd rather not have the two of them slinging fists in front of the woman who just called me a tramp. "*My* mother does have an appointment in a few hours and it's going to take a chunk of that time to get her cleaned up and in the car, so let me walk you to your vehicle, Luke. You look like you're on your way to work, anyway."

He comes with me a little less willingly than I'd like but we reach his vehicle and I shift my weight on the gravel that's digging into my bare feet. I pull Luke's shoulders around so he's facing me instead of the house where Conner is standing on the porch like he owns the place. I wish he did. Then I'd wipe that smug smile off his face with a bill for what the repairs to the house are going to cost and save myself from worrying about what to do with Mom now that Rusty is dead. Whoever he left this house to is probably going to kick her out in favor of demolishing the place. I'm sure bulldozing it will be cheaper than doing mold remediation. "Nothing is going on between Conner and me," I tell Luke. "I'm pretty sure he showed up here this morning just to beat you here, and I would really appreciate it if the two of you would stop trying to use me to tick each other off." I let go of him. "I'm not a prop to be used in your feud, and don't tell me that's not what you're doing because Jan told me..."

The words die in my throat. I'm not sure why talking about babies is suddenly making me mournful. The muscles in Luke's jaw tick. "Jan and Abbie get along great, so I'm sure Jan did tell you a few things. As far as I'm concerned, whatever she said has nothing to do with me. Abbie made her own decisions the same way Conner did. The same way you are." He looks beyond me to the house again. "I'm not the one using you as a prop. Believe that or not, and forgive me if I don't believe you straight away when you say there's nothing going on between you and him. I've been lied to before, and he was at the center of it all."

I press my hand to Luke's chest, getting his attention back on me. "Which is why I'm not lying to you now."

He tucks a strand of hair behind my ear. "No, you're just trying to tell me that my motives aren't what I know they are."

I swallow. He's sounding more like a guy who's just trying to date a girl rather than the interrogating cop from moments ago. I'd like to keep it that way, but I also want to know what his true motives are. Is he setting me up for B's crimes because doing so will hurt Conner? For that to be true, Luke has to believe that Conner actually does have feelings for me. I collect my thoughts and focus on heading off any actions Conner has taken that would lead Luke to believe I'm the object of his rival's affection. "Conner and I are talking through what happened in the history we have together, but I promise you, he did *not* spend the night here. He's just trying to get a rise out of you because you apparently bragged all over town about me making biscuits for you. That's why I don't know if you want to go pretending that your motives are all pure toward me. That doesn't seem to be the case, and biscuits are a stupid thing for two grown men to fight about."

Luke wipes his face, making the grin trying to sprout on his lips disappear. "You're right. I made those biscuits into an issue because Conner was standing around acting like he's somebody when he's not even a volunteer fireman. Conner mows lawns for a living. That's how he snaked his way in with my wife. I hired him, thinking he was a friend who could use the money, but what he took was my wife." He stares at me, using his cop face again. "I drove by here last night. Conner's truck was here then, parked exactly where it is right now. Explain that to me because I kept driving last night, but this morning I needed to talk to you. About why I ran off on you yesterday. The explosion at Rusty's."

My heart was just beginning to calm down, but now it's firing back up again. I rub my palms on the little bit of shirt covering my stomach and glance to where Conner is no longer smiling. "Yeah, he was here last night. I don't know where he parked exactly, but he did come by to help me with something."

"What did he help you with?" Luke asks.

I run my bare toes over the sharp gravel I can now barely feel beneath my feet. I'll feel it after the adrenaline drains from my system. "Rusty is...*was* the closest thing my mom had to a friend. Conner used to help me with her when she was drunk, so he knows about her dependency on Talico Bar. He came by to see if I needed help breaking the news of Rusty's death to her."

Luke studies me as if he's trying to figure out what I'm lying about. Or maybe he already knows the parts I'm lying about and he's just waiting for me to confess. I motion to the house. "I know I had a disagreement with Rusty, but look at this place. Surely no one can blame me for asking him to fix it up. *Asking* him to be a decent landlord and him refusing doesn't lead to murder. I left the bar thinking about how to get Mom to move into a new place, not about trying to blow up Rusty's house."

Luke's eyes narrow. "Who said you were a suspect?"

I clear my throat. "No one. I mean, well, Conner brought up my having been at Talico Bar..."

Luke looks at Conner. "So that's why he was here last night. He ran here to tell you that I gave an official statement about what happened in Rusty's bar the other night." He drops his gaze back to mine. "Is Conner trying to coerce you into saying things that aren't true? That I started the fight, not him?"

I shake my head. "No, nothing even close to that. He really was here helping me break the news to my mom, then he mentioned that you mentioned my argument with Rusty, which really wasn't an argument at all…" I clamp my mouth shut, the nervous way my words are rambling out sounding suspicious even to my own ears.

Luke opens his door. "Okay, I've got to work a double shift today and I doubt there will be much downtime, so I better get going."

The abrupt departure worries me. I cup the edge of his door and apologize, even for the things I'm not certain of. "I'm sorry, Luke. For what Conner's presence here looks like, and for everything you've gone through."

He pulls in a long breath and exhales slowly. "I really hope you're being as honest with me as I'm being with you, Sierra, because I'm here for you, for as little or as long as you're in Poca. If you only have eyes for Conner, that's fine. Just let me know so I can wish you good luck with that because Conner has eyes for everyone." He drops into his seat. "If he's a part of your life, I can't be." Luke tugs on his door and I step away from the vehicle. He slams his door shut, revs his already running engine, and backs out of the driveway.

Conner crunches over the gravel behind me, his arm sliding around my waist and his cheek pressing against mine. "Good girl. Now let's get you out of my shirt and into something I'm going to like a whole lot less."

~16~

I fidget with the hem of my long-sleeve shirt. I'm not sure if Luke paid any attention to the marks on my arms the way Conner did, but despite summer's warm embrace, I'm once again forced to hide fresh scratches. Mom didn't want a bath today. I haven't been forcing her to shower every day, though I have insisted that she run a washcloth over her important bits. This morning, she was having none of any of it. When I tried to force her into the tub, explaining that her greasy hair needed to be washed before she could see the doctor, she attacked with all the ferocity of a lioness. If Conner hadn't barreled through the door when he did, I'd have more than two thick bloody trails of claw marks down my arms.

Slightly more mortifying than Conner having to save me from getting my tail beat by an old drunk is the fact that ever since his front-row seat to the action, he's been distant. No eye contact, and the only words he's spoken to me are the ones he used to insist that I get into his truck because he was driving us to Mom's doctor's appointment. I said no, but

Mom is clinging to him like he's *her* hero, as if I'm the one who was at fault for having the audacity to want her clean before the doctor's visit.

I guess I shouldn't be surprised that Mom is choosing someone over me. The real issue is riding in Conner's shotgun seat, sitting next to a man who's hot one minute and cold the next. He showed me just enough of the old Conner this morning to sway my heart back in his favor. I nearly even forgot that he accused me of murder just last night.

I look down at my sandals. I might look dopey in my choice of a baggy V-neck and capris, but my shoes are cute. And at least no one else in Poca will ever see me wearing what Conner and Luke did this morning. I threw that rag of a t-shirt into the garbage and chucked my shorts in behind it. I want no reminder of the humiliation of being caught in a shirt I should have thrown away years ago.

Conner pulls into the medical park that's an unfortunate hour away from Mom's house. Not a word has been uttered since we pulled out of her driveway. My body tenses as he circles the lot for a parking spot. When Mom was fighting me earlier, she called me Valerie again. Even after Conner got her calmed down, she acted as if she had no idea who I was. I thought she was only trying to annoy me but Conner pointed out that there was real fear in her eyes. I saw it then and tried to talk to her about it, but she flipped out on me again. Conner's was the only voice she would respond to. She spoke to him with a softness I never get from her.

He pulls into a spot two rows away from the door and I hurry out of the truck. If Mom still refuses to acknowledge me or throws a tantrum, I'll have to let Conner take her inside. The idea of having to rely on him infuriates me. I slam the door and move to the extended cab where Mom is, gently opening her door to find her snoring softly. I should have guessed that the reason she's been quiet is because she's asleep, but I also figured that maybe she was back here grumbling and I just couldn't hear her over the noise of the truck engine and the scream of the heavy metal music Conner had playing.

He rounds the truck and stretches an arm past my waist and over Mom's lap, unbuckling her before I get the chance. "Like a kid," he mutters. "When you want to put them to sleep, buckle them into a car seat and go for a drive."

I shoulder him away, taking control of the seatbelt as it slides into place along the side of the seat. "Sounds like you're ready for your mistress's child to be born. Good for you. Luke is going to love sharing Daddy duties with you. Feel free to get some more practice and go for another drive while I take *my* mother inside for her doctor's appointment." I gently rub her arm. "Hey, sleepy lady. We're here. How are you feeling?"

Her eyes spring open and she looks past me to Conner. He reaches over me and puts a hand on her shoulder, stretching his other long arm into the bed of the truck. He lifts Mom's cane out of the back and hip-checks me, forcing me to step away from the door. "I'm not inclined to let you out of my sight, Sierra, so I'll help her inside and sit in the waiting room until you two are finished up." He nods to the handicap spots. "She needs a sticker. Put that on your list next to the new toaster."

I dig my nails into my hand to keep from slapping the jerk. "Why don't you bring her your toaster? Or better yet, move her into your place. I'm sure the two of you will be *very* happy together, and Aunt Di will stop by from time to time. Her husband is in a wheelchair and I'm sure she'll let you borrow his handicap permit anytime you lovebirds need it."

After what happened in the bathroom, I shouldn't have this much of an attitude with him, but I've already thanked him for the help and now he's purposefully being obnoxious. I'm only returning the favor. Besides, today has been another steady stream of horror and it's barely gotten started. I don't need Conner in my face while I deal with my mom and process the fact that there's possibly a sick psycho out drowning cars and burning men alive. I might miss the parts of Conner that are familiar, but I nearly kissed him this morning after he got Mom settled into the bath. I can't afford to make those kinds of mistakes. Not after also nearly sleeping with Luke. Whether or not anything Conner or Luke has ever said to me is true, I need to shut both of them down before they gain whatever rumor-spreading leverage they're after.

I wait for Conner to get Mom out of the truck and steadied on her feet. He slips the cane into her palm, handling her as if she's liable to break at any second. She looks up at him with gap-toothed admiration. "Thank you, handsome. You're nice and solid, I like that."

I fold my arms over my chest. "Would you two like me to leave you alone? Or maybe you want me to rent a room for you? From what I recall, an hour should more than cover it."

Conner's blue eyes flick with anger. "What I'd like is for you to stop being petty."

I snatch Mom's hand away from him. "The way you're not being petty with Luke and using me to do it? No thanks." I whirl Mom away from him, too slowly for the action to really make a statement. "You've known Conner all of my life, Mom. You never liked him before, so don't go falling for him now."

He strolls up on the other side of her, gripping her elbow. "We're turning over a new leaf, Sierra. Your mom and I are going to be best friends. Especially since I'm going to be glued to you from here on out. So yeah, I'll bring over the toaster from my place."

I stare a hole through the side of his face. "What is your problem?"

He slides his eyes to mine. "The fact that you even have to ask me that question is my problem."

I blow out an irritated huff. "Yeah, well, you always had better things to do before and I'm sure it won't be long until even the dullest of things in Poca takes you right back out of our door, so don't make her promises you'll never live up to."

His fist slams against the button for the handicap entrance and the doors to the medical building slide slowly open. I hasten Mom inside, navigating to the neurologist's waiting room. When Mom was in the hospital last, Aunt Di said the doctor there recommended she see a neurologist. I started working on getting her this appointment before I ever left Dallas.

Conner lets go of Mom's elbow and plops himself into the first empty seat in the waiting room. I take Mom to the front with me, sitting her in a chair right beside the reception desk. "Hello, I'm Sierra Clifton. My mother Wanda Clifton has an appointment."

The dark-haired receptionist hands me a clipboard. "You've filled out most of the paperwork online but I'll need your mother to sign these." She looks beside me. "Is she able to consent? Or do you have a medical power of attorney?"

I look down at the forms and say a prayer that Mom will sign without kicking up a fuss. Mainly because I don't want Conner to rush up here and save the stinking day again. "She can consent."

~17~

D r. Sparks is younger than I expected. For some reason, that's all I can focus on while words spill out of his mouth with an even cadence. There's a gray patch of hair by his ears so that must mean he's older than his youthful face is willing to admit. I wonder if the gastroenterologist will be the same? That's the next appointment on our list. I only started with the neurologist because assessing a brain issue seemed to be a bit more important than Mom's GI problems. Now, I'm not so sure. I'd rather not hear what Dr. Sparks is saying.

"Miss Clifton?" His brows knit together and before I start counting the hairs in each bushy row, I clear my throat.

"Sorry, this is just a lot to take in."

He offers me a grim smile. "I know. That's why I asked you to step out into the hallway with me, there's no point in worrying your mother any further. I do need you to be honest in answering my questions though. Is your mother typically this combative with you?"

I cup a hand over my opposite arm and slowly pull up my sleeve, uncomfortable with the truth I'm trying to hide. "My whole life, she's lived in a constate state of being agitated with me, so that part is normal. What you just saw in the examination room is tame, though, compared to the episodes she's been having lately. These fresh scratches are from this morning. She fought me like I was Satan trying to drag her into Hell when I was only trying to wash her hair."

He scans the marks on my arms. "You mentioned that you haven't been around a lot in recent years. Since you've been back, is your mother's behavior toward you worse, better, or the same as when you left?"

I lower my sleeve. "I'd have to say her behavior is just...different. Before, she didn't fight me, she'd just hit me."

"Was this abuse happening daily?" he asks.

I shrug, choosing my words carefully so I don't get stuck reliving the details. "Sometimes. But she mostly left me alone as long as I didn't get in her way or bug her about anything. The only time she really came after me was if I dumped out her alcohol. Back then, she could get around though, so she always managed to get more liquor. Now, she's too weak to go out on her own."

He nods. "How long has it been since she reached this point where she can't get around on her own?"

Embarrassment colors my cheeks. "I'm not entirely sure. After I left home, my aunt was the one checking on Mom but Aunt Diana didn't really monitor whether or not Mom was going out or having someone bring alcohol to her. She did tell me that a local bar owner was bringing Mom bottles of liquor every week, but he's not doing that anymore." My pulse quickens, all too aware that Rusty is now permanently removed from Mom's life. "She can't drive and you can see that she barely walks, so it's hard to say if her temper is worse now, or if she's only triggered because I dumped out every single bit of alcohol she has. I made her go cold turkey. Was that the wrong thing to do?"

He crosses an arm along his chest and props his other elbow on it, fingers caressing the bottom of his chin. "She shouldn't be drinking with the medication she's on, and she shouldn't be forgetting who you are. Not even with the years of absence you mentioned. She was calling you Valerie. Do you know anyone with that name? Someone she could be confusing you with. Another sibling?"

I shake my head. "She occasionally called me Valerie when I was kid. I don't know why. I just got used to answering to any name she yelled."

He nods, like he's fitting all the pieces of Mom's wiring together. "I'm going to recommend that she see a psychiatrist. Alcoholism usually develops for a reason and your mother's outbursts and usage of the wrong name could be connected to experiences she's had that are unresolved."

"Okay," I whisper, the weight of me being the reason Mom drinks pressing against my lungs.

Dr. Sparks drops his hand from his chin and places it on my shoulder. "I know this has been tough to hear, but I do think it's very possible your mother is suffering from early onset dementia. I'll order the scans and follow the data, but an alcoholic developing this condition isn't unheard of. If this is in fact the case, she'll need a medical power of attorney. Consider whether or not you want to take on that role because if your mother is diagnosed, I'm sorry to tell you that what I just saw transpire in that room could very well be the tip of the iceberg."

Tears prick my eyes. My expectations for this appointment were low. I expected Mom to have cognitive difficulties due to the alcohol abuse, but I wasn't prepared for a permanent cognitive deterioration. "Miss Clifton?" Dr. Sparks questions. "Did you want to go back inside while I finish up with your mom? We're almost done, so you can wait out front if you prefer."

My body feels heavy, like my blood is turning to stone. "I'll wait in the reception area. If you need help walking her out, let me know and I'll send my friend. She likes him."

The doctor nods in understanding. "I'll order the tests and have one of the nurses call you when they're scheduled."

He reenters Mom's room and I turn away from the door. I walk out into the lobby and automatically weave my heavy limbs through the chairs to Conner. Maybe he's as comforting to me as he is to Mom. I sit down next to him, my eyes straight ahead, trained on nothing. Conner dips his head forward, trying to intercept my unseeing gaze. "So? How's she doing?"

I give him the short answer. "She's a diabetic alcoholic whose kidneys are failing, and now she's having memory loss."

He leans back, relaxing into his chair. "She's not the only person around here whose memory is bad."

I spin on him. "Dementia, Conner. She probably has dementia, which is a heck of a lot worse than your terrible memory about what our relationship actually was."

He huffs. "My bad memory? You're the one walking around here, free as a bird, like nothing ever happened."

I lift from my seat and storm out of the doctor's office. Conner follows me. I flick a hand at him in warning. "Don't. I want to be alone."

He doesn't listen. He cuts me off and pulls me into his arms. "I'm sorry. Dementia is a big deal and I shouldn't have taken a jab at you right after you got that kind of news."

I shove him away from me. "Take as many jabs as you like because we are not dating. We are not a couple. So keep showing me your true colors while you stop acting like you care about me *or* my mom. I've had enough of your mood swings. You're not happy to see me and we can just leave it at that."

He shoves his hands into his pockets. "I lied to you."

I throw my eyes open wide with sarcasm. "Yeah, I know."

He blows out a breath. "No, you don't. Because when you're wrong, you never admit it. I do. Which is why I lied about never looking for you." His eyes shift to the left and then back again. "It took me a while, but I tracked you down. I came to Texas. Twice. The last time was about a year ago. I followed you from your apartment all the way to your job, and I watched you all week long, coming and going." His head dips. "You looked like you were doing okay so I left without confronting you. I didn't want to rain on your parade, so to speak. I came back here, wrecked all over again because you were gone and I was here. That's when the whole Luke's wife thing happened." He looks at me. "I was hurting and I needed someone, Sierra. You weren't here and I...just needed someone."

My heart thuds. If I knew Conner wanted me in his life, I would have reached out to him. Despite how placating I was when we were together, Conner was always kind to me and I loved him in a way I'll never truly be able to let go of. I move toward him but my phone rings, a sound I so rarely hear it makes me jump. I dig the device out of my pocket. "Sorry. The doctor's probably looking for me. I told him I'd be in the lobby." I swipe the screen and answer the call. "Hello?" It isn't the doctor or any of his staff. It's Luke. "Sure. Okay, I'll be there."

I end the call and meet Conner's waiting stare. "That was Luke. He just made an official request for me to come to the police station."

Conner shakes his head. "You're not doing that. Tell him no."

I sigh. "I just told him I would. It isn't about Rusty anyway. Luke said I need to make a statement about what transpired at Talico Bar the night you started a fight with him."

Conner's jaw works. "If he wants a statement, I'll give it. Not you. Tell Luke Putnam anything he has to say to you can be said through me."

~*18*~

Conner's just as quiet on the ride back to Mom's house as he was on the way to Dr. Sparks'. I'm glad for the silence. A lot has been dumped on my lap today and I need time to process what's happening in my life, and everyone else's. Mom's frailty now has a new meaning. While the alcohol is her own fault and the constant drinking might have hastened in the dementia, she can't be blamed for the deterioration of her mind. If Dr. Sparks' testing confirms what he suspected today, a power of attorney will have to be appointed for Mom and I need to unpack how I feel about that person being me. Signing on for such a thing means I'm with her for the rest of her life. She gave birth to me when she was only nineteen so for all I know, she could live another fifty years. Already, at forty-seven, she's in need of daily care. Care I'll be solely responsible for if I sign those papers.

On top of Mom's eternal care, I have to trudge through what Conner spewed all over me in the parking lot. Not only the part where he wants me to make Luke think I approve of Conner being my spokesperson, but the part where he claims he was in Texas. Twice. Hunting me down only to watch me from the shadows like B described doing in the diary. Conner watched me but never spoke to me. Never let me know he was heartbroken the same way I was. All he's done is blame me for all the bad parts of his life, and now that includes his affair with Luke's wife. I'm the cause of all his woes and that's about as fair as me being stuck taking care of a mother who'd rather spit on me than let me help her into a chair.

As if none of that is enough, I now also have my impending meeting with Luke to figure out. I'm not sure what he meant by *official statement*. He was there during the fight with Conner and Luke's word on what happened should carry more weight than anything I could add. Especially since the fight had to do with his wife and not me. "I'm going to the meeting with Luke."

Conner keeps his focus on the road ahead of us. "Luke is using the fight as a ploy to get you into the police station so he can question you about..." he glances into his rearview and then over at me, "The explosion."

Despite being appreciative of his discretion not to mention Rusty by name, seeing how I haven't yet told Mom that her one friend is dead, a fresh wound opens inside my heart. "Which is why I'm going to the police station. You think I'm capable of such a thing, and maybe Luke does too. There's only one way to find out, and one way to prove I'm not."

Conner opens his console and retrieves a bottle of aspirin. "What if Luke is? Because if he's the one behind it, then you're getting ready to become either his scapegoat or his alibi."

I shrug. "I'm neither of those things and the evidence will prove it."

"Fine," he grumbles, tossing back two aspirin and swallowing them down dry. "I'll go to the station with you. Then—" He slams on his brakes, staring at the row of vehicles lined along the railroad tracks that wind back in behind the trailer court we grew up in.

I glance at the machinery sitting on the tracks next to the vehicles. "Looks like they're getting ready to replace the rails. Or at least the timbers underneath them." I point to a stack of railroad ties lying beside one of the white railroad vehicles.

Conner glares at me. "Thank you for stating the freaking obvious."

He hits the gas and I grab the little handle above my head, cranking my neck to make sure Mom is still buckled nicely into her seat. She is, and she's staring at the back of Conner's head like the man who owns that messy hair walks on water. "Get a room," I mumble under my breath and right my posture. I let go of the handle and immediately decide better of it. Conner is driving like he's racing to a fire and as Luke has already pointed out, Conner is no fireman. "Where's the emergency, Conner? I'm sure the railroad crew isn't going to pillage the community. Though maybe they should bulldoze the trailer court." I shoot him a look, hand tight on the oh-crap bar. "Wait, do you still live there? Are you worried they're going to mess with your property?"

He cuts onto a bumpy side street and doesn't bother slowing down until Mom yelps from behind me. He curses under his breath and taps his antsy fingers over the steering wheel. "Yeah, I still live there. I bought a new trailer a while back but I figured I might as well stay right there." He glances at me with narrowed eyes. "Close to the scene of the crime. Just in case anyone decided to come back to Poca."

His words shock me as much as his declaration about being in Dallas did. "You waited there? For me?"

"Stop flattering yourself." He cuts back onto the main road and picks up speed. "I've got a few errands to run but don't go to the police station without me. I'll be back to pick you up in a couple of hours."

I mark the sign of the cross over my chest. "If we happen to make it back to Mom's house in one piece, I'll drive myself to the meeting I was summoned to because of you."

He skids to a stop outside of Mom's house, not bothering to pull into the driveway. "You'll wait for me, and that's final." He jumps out of the truck and races around to Mom's door, cradling her in his arms before I scramble myself out of my seat. "Hurry up!" he yells over his shoulder as he sprints to the door.

I slam his truck door for the second time and retrieve Mom's cane from the truck bed. I walk to the front door like a normal person and unlock it. He glares at me the whole time. "I'm going to put your mom in her room, and then I'm leaving. When I get back, you better be here."

~

The uniformed officer from the front desk of the police station escorts me to a small room slightly behind and off to the left of where she was seated when I came in. There's a couch, two plush chairs, and a coffee table running at an angle between the seating arrangements. The officer waves her hand around the crowded space. "Sit anywhere you like. Sergeant Putnam will be with you shortly."

"Okay, thanks." I walk deeper into the room and sit where I imagine they prefer their suspects to sit. On the couch. I texted Luke to tell him I was on my way and thought maybe he'd be waiting outside to greet me. He didn't respond to my message, though, and now that I'm sitting in this fluffed-up version of an interrogation room, I think Conner might have been right. I'm not here about the fight he started with Luke. I'm here to be implicated in Rusty's murder.

My head begins to pound. I shouldn't be nervous, not with today's technology. Despite what Luke or anyone else says, surely Rusty had surveillance on his bar. As soon as the police check the cameras, they'll see that I left and never came back. Plus, my cell phone was in my car that night, inside my big bag of a purse that I didn't take into the bar with me. When I got back to Mom's, I put my phone on my nightstand to use it for a clock. I didn't set an alarm because I usually don't need one, I'm a naturally early riser, but I'm sure something in the phone's data will confirm its location on my nightstand.

The door opens and Luke walks in, a man an inch shorter than him following on his heels. "Hi." Luke gives me one of his effortless smiles. "Thanks for coming. This is Detective Brown. He has some questions for you, and then we'll let you get back to your mom."

I tamp down my suspicion about Luke and meet Detective Brown's unimpressive brown eyes, giving the man a greeting nod. "Hello. Nice to meet you."

He sits in the chair to my right and extends his hand over the table. "Nice to meet you as well. Can I get you anything? A soda pop or a bag of chips?"

I give his hand a shake and release it as quickly as possible. "No, thanks. I had a late lunch right before I came over here."

That's a lie. I was too nervous to eat, but they don't need to know that. Luke sits in the chair to my left and leans his arms onto his legs. "How's your mom? Did the doctor's appointment go okay?"

I rub the back of my neck. "Not exactly. She's maybe dealing with some things I wasn't aware of. We won't know for sure until some more testing is done."

"That doesn't sound good," Detective Brown states casually. "What type of things do you think she's maybe dealing with?"

I stiffen. This man is anything but casual. He's digging. My eyes dart to Luke, who nods and smiles like this is no big deal and I should go ahead and answer the question. My hackles rise. I look at my arms, to where my shirt is covering the fresh scratches. I wonder if Luke noticed the old ones after all. He might have me here to photograph the healing marks he saw this morning. As far as Conner said, Rusty was blown up. Maybe he fought with someone before they torched his double-wide, though. If so, he'd have *their* skin under his nails, not mine. Technology and science are still on my side. DNA tests will prove it wasn't me. "Um, my mom's health is kind of hard to talk about."

Detective Brown flips open his notepad, clicking the top of his ballpoint pen. "What doctor did she see today?"

I swallow. "Dr. Sparks."

He looks up to the corner of the room. "I'm not familiar. Is he local?"

I shrug. "He's outside of Poca city limits but only about forty-five minutes from the police station here, so fairly local."

Luke shifts a little more forward. "Is he your mom's primary doctor?"

I look between the two men. "No, he's a neurologist. After Mom's last trip to the hospital, her primary care doctor told my Aunt Di...Diana, that Mom needed to see a neurologist, so I started working on getting her in with one before I even got to Poca."

Detective Brown writes in his notebook. "And the news Dr. Sparks gave you today was bad news?"

I rub my sweaty palms over the dress slacks I changed into before coming here. "Like I said, nothing is certain yet. He's sending her for more testing and recommended that I also get her into some therapy sessions with a psychologist, but he does think it's possible that Mom has early onset dementia."

I glance at Luke again, not sure if he's filled Detective Brown in on the state of my mom's alcoholism. I wouldn't be surprised if he's picked her up for public intoxication in the years since I left here and he became an officer. He just smiles at me. "Don't be nervous. You're doing fine. We just needed to have you come answer some questions for us."

"I won't keep you long," Detective Brown adds. "Conner Ferguson drove you to Dr. Sparks' office today?"

My eyes snap to his, a prickly sensation setting off all of my alarm bells. "He did."

"Are the two of you in a relationship?" the detective asks.

I shift, crossing my legs at the ankles. "Not a romantic one, if that's what you mean by relationship."

"Friends then?" he continues.

I clear my throat. "Until recently, I hadn't spoken to Conner in a lot of years. What happened at Talico Bar was more about..." I look at Luke.

He sits up and tugs his arms off of his legs. "Detective Brown knows about my wife's affair with Mr. Ferguson. So just answer his questions, and we'll get this whole thing put behind us."

I uncross my ankles, feeling the urge not only to defend myself, but Conner. "I'm honestly not sure what I would consider Conner Ferguson, Detective. I guess you would say it's complicated, but not in a romantically entangled way. We dated as teens, and then I left Poca without saying goodbye to him." Luke sucks in a sharp breath. I do my best to ignore the widening of his eyes. "I didn't give Conner closure, so that's why he's hanging around and driving my mom to doctor's appointments. To talk through things and put our past to rest, not to rekindle it."

Detective Brown scribbles in his notebook. "After the fight at Talico Bar, did Mr. Ferguson come by your place to *hang* out?"

My face burns. "No, he didn't."

The detective flips to a new page. "After the fight, when did you next speak to Mr. Ferguson?"

I close my eyes, trying to remember. "The next day, I think. That evening. He came by to tell me what happened with the explosion." I open my eyes. "Rusty was a friend of my mom's, and Conner knew that."

I've told this lie once already, so now I have to stick with it. The detective shifts forward. "Do you know where Mr. Ferguson was between the time you last saw him at Talico Bar and when he arrived at your house the next evening?"

I stare into his steady brown eyes. I wasn't summoned here because they think *I* blew up Rusty's place. They called me here because they think Conner did. Or because instead of framing me, Luke is going to frame Conner? "No, I have no idea where Conner was, but..."

"But what?" the man pressures.

I clasp my hands together. "I don't know who Conner is today, but I do know who he was. The Conner Ferguson I knew would never, ever, do anything to hurt another person."

"He's not that same boy anymore, Sierra," Luke confirms, sitting in front of me as living proof that Conner in fact *will* hurt people. But sex and murder and two very different things.

Detective Brown places his hand on the table. "Let me ask you something. Kaity Bell Edwards left Poca around the same time you did. For a while, people said the two of you had run off together. Did you?"

"Kaity?" My head swims, visions of the glitter-crusted Ks plastered all over town floating through my mind. "No. We weren't friends. I mean, I knew her, and she was friends with Luke and Conner, but I never hung out with her unless I was with Conner. I didn't even know Kaity ran away until recently."

"Hmm," the detective muses. "What makes you think she ran away?"

My spine goes erect. I blink at what he's implying. "I...just assumed." I look to Luke. "Is that not what happened?"

There's a knock on the door. The detective reaches back and opens it. "Yeah?"

The officer from the front desk purses her lips. "Conner Ferguson is here. He says Miss Clifton is needed at home. Urgently."

Luke scans my face. "You told him you were coming here?"

I nod, getting off the sofa. "He was sitting next to me when you called. We were still at the doctor's office. I better go see what's happened."

Luke blocks my path. "You stay right here. I'll go see what's going on, and I'll get you home if there's a reason for it, but I highly doubt it."

<h1 style="text-align:center">~ 19 ~</h1>

Unease is rattling every nerve in my body. Luke's request for me to stay inside this cozy attempt at an interrogation room was polite enough on the surface, but the sentiment was clear. I'm not free to go. If that's the case, any number of my worst fears could be true.

Raised voices shatter through the silence of the interrogation room. I recognize Conner's above all the others. He sounds like his patience is as far gone as my own. I leave my seat and open the door, stepping out into the hall. Conner is straight ahead, at the mouth of the hallway beside the desk, ignoring every order from the four cops around him. His eyes lock onto mine. "Come here, Sierra."

Luke turns to find me standing outside the room he left me in. "Stay there, Sierra."

Conner's teeth grind. "Come. Here."

I take a step toward him but Luke puts his arm out to stop me. "He's on his way to being arrested for obstruction. You don't want to get yourself dragged into it."

Conner lifts his hands in the air to show the officers around him that he's not a threat. "What am I obstructing? You? Sorry to break it to you, but Sierra is no more interested in you than Abbie is."

Luke lunges for Conner. Detective Brown cuts him off and shoves Conner out of the way, pushing him into the paws of one of the other officers while Brown swings around and yanks Luke's collar. "Take a walk. Cool off."

Luke's nostrils flare. He straightens his shirt and holds a hand out to me. "Want to take a walk?"

I know what he's asking and it has nothing to do with spending time with me. He wants me to take a stand for him, right now, in front of Conner and everyone else. How can I? Even if he's not trying to frame Conner or me for murder, there's still his pregnant wife to consider. I shake my head, sorrow filling my chest. "I can't. I need to go home. Mom's been in bad shape today, her mind all over the place, and Conner was watching her for me. If he says I need to get home to her, then that's where I need to go."

Luke's hand falls and his eyes harden in a way I've never seen from him. "You're not done here, which is why I told you to stay put."

"Is she under arrest?" Conner barks. "I didn't think so. You have no right to detain her. Let's go, Sierra."

I take a chance on moving past Luke. He doesn't attempt to stop me so I keep walking, straight to where Conner is being corralled. I lower my voice and hope he can hear the message I'm trying to send. "I came here of my own free will and I'm leaving on it too, because they don't want to question me about anything other than *you*."

Conner's expression goes blank. He looks over my head. "Instead of you people harassing Sierra, how about you question me? I'll gladly go on record to tell everyone how I punched Sergeant Putnam in his womanizing face."

There's scuffling behind me but Conner doesn't let me turn around. He moves forward, wrapping one arm around my back and pulling me to his chest, his mouth close to mine as he whispers. "He called you a canary for a reason. He's expecting you to sing."

I look up into his eyes. "About what? I don't know anything about you, him, or Rusty."

He rests his forehead on mine. "I know. So go on home. Your mom needs her dinner soon, and I doubt she wants me operating her broken toaster." He presses a kiss to the top of my head and releases me. "Go. Now."

~

I stare out the window above the kitchen sink. The thick film of scum on it makes everything outside look distorted. Even the burgundy-haired little girl who's staring back at me. She's at the edge of the thin line of trees that hide where the utility easement runs behind the house. The gas company keeps that area clear so the child must be using the easy access of the easement to spy on me. Or all of the neighbors. Maybe her appearance isn't connected to the diary at all. Maybe she's only a snoop and I'm being paranoid. What type of person would send a kid to plant a diary inside of a rotting window seat in a room no one could know I would search in the first place? Furthermore, why would anyone choose a dilapidated house like this one to hide anything in? None of this makes sense. Not the diary's pristine condition standing in direct contrast to where I found it, or this somber-faced kid watching me from the shadows.

I shiver as a light breeze ruffles the trees around the girl, making her appearance even creepier. I watch her watching me, tracing the hint of familiarity in her features. Maybe she's the kid of someone I went to school with. *B's* kid. The floor behind me creaks. I drop the cup I'm washing and spin around with a squeak. Conner leans on the doorframe. "It's just me."

I flip a hand into the air, sending soapy suds splattering across my face. "Just you? Breaking into my house and sneaking up on me?"

He shoves off the frame and walks toward me. "I didn't break in. I took your mom's house key earlier."

I back into the sink. "That's no better."

He drags a hand towel off the counter, his chest expanding and softly falling as he reaches out and dabs the soapy suds off my face. "It's been a really long day. Let's not fight anymore." He tosses the towel back onto the counter. "I took the key because she doesn't need it, and because I love you so much more than I can ever hate you. I didn't want to admit that. Not out loud anyway, because I know I shouldn't feel this way about you." He brings his hand up to cup my face, staring into my eyes. "You have *always* been my priority. I might not be happy about that anymore, but I can't stop putting you above everyone else. Even myself."

My throat tightens. As painful and confusing as Conner is, his actions at the police station were protective. I don't know why, especially since the protectiveness was unnecessary. Maybe he reacted that way for the exact same reason I also felt the need to protect him. Love. Maybe

Conner was trying to prove he does, or did, love me. "I never asked you to put me first."

He breathes in deeply, as if inhaling all the air I just exhaled. "I know you didn't ask, and I was a crummy boyfriend because of it. I thought we had an understanding and by the time I realized we didn't, you'd ruined everything."

Tears hasten their way into my eyes. "I've heard you loud and clear. I'm the cause of every bad thing that's ever happened in your entire life, so just leave the key on the counter and walk away."

He tilts my head back, bringing our lips closer together. "You're the cause of the *worst* things that have happened in my life, and before that, you were the cause of the absolute best. I'll never be able to walk away from you. So meet me in this space, Sierra. Right here where nothing is okay, but we're together despite it. I want to be whole again, and to do that I need you." His lips brush mine. "Make these last eleven years worth all the hell you put me through."

His words melt inside me. I clutch his shirt. "Me kissing you won't take away the pain. It might feel good for now, but later, you're still going to despise me more than you like me."

He runs his hand from my face to my shoulder, dragging it slowly down to rest on my hip. His other hand follows suit. He hoists me onto the edge of the sink, his hands continuing to trace down my body, gliding over my thighs until he's cupped underneath them and wrapping them around his waist. He fits himself against me. "It's going to feel good now *and* later, because you're going to talk to me the whole time, telling me how you feel and what you're thinking. Then you're going to give me a chance to set the record straight because you keep things twisted in this beautiful head of yours." He runs his fingers along my cheek. "I adore you. I always have. And the pain that comes with loving you this much is the kind of pain I don't ever want to forget because to get over it means letting go of you, and I can't do that." His mouth covers mine. I don't fight it. Conner sparks desire in me like no one else ever has. No matter what I tell myself or anyone else, I'll *always* be entangled with Conner. Romantically, and in every other way there is.

He lifts me off the sink and carries me through the house to the stairs, breaking our kiss as he walks us slowly up them. "Look at me," he whispers when we reach the top. I cup his face in my hands and stare into his eyes. He doesn't smile. His hands only tighten where he's holding me to him. "I want every part of you, Sierra. The inside as much as the outside. Every thought. Every feeling. Every desire. All of you. From this day until my last."

~*20*~

Lying next to Conner is surreal. I feel like even taking a breath will break the spell we're under, so I'd rather not need air because I don't want to leave this moment. I don't want to face any other part of reality. This life, right here in his arms, is the only one I ever want to have. He rolls onto his side and I groan. He mocks the sound, propping himself up on his elbow, looking down at me and tracing a finger along the curve of my jaw. "We're incredible together. Not because it's been so long or because we were each other's first. We're only this good together because we're a perfect match."

I swallow. "Then why are you getting up?"

His finger smooths its way across my lips. "I'm not. I just want to see your face when I'm talking to you, so I can watch for all the little things you might be thinking but not telling me." He lowers down and kisses me. "The only thing I don't want you to tell me is details about anyone else you've been with. I don't want to know who you dated after you left because all that matters to me is knowing that I've had the best of you. The same as you've had of me. The people who got us in the middle don't matter. They can't. Not when I can look into your eyes the way I just did and *know* that no one has ever satisfied you the way I do. Thank you for giving me that, Sierra. I always tried before, to work at pleasing you the way you worked at it for me, but I was just a boy pretending to be a man for you. Thank you for letting the man I've become have a shot at treating you right."

I study the harsh lines of his face. The sharp angles he had as a boy are now the planes of a man's equally handsome face. "You weren't ever shy about *anything*, so yeah, I did see you as more man than boy. Maybe that's why I didn't want to tell you about all the childish thoughts in my head." I run my hand over his abs. "I'm sorry I left you."

He sighs. "What's done is done. Now we only need to make sure that history doesn't repeat itself. What did you say to Detective Brown today?"

I sit up, pulling the bed sheet over my chest and tucking it in place with my bent knees. "Nothing. He was digging for answers about you, wanting to know if I knew where you were between the time you and Luke fought to the time you showed up here the next evening." I chew on my lip. "You didn't do something stupid, did you?"

He sits up and slides against the headboard, pulling me back to rest on his chest. "Doing stupid things is your department. Meaning no, I didn't have anything to do with Rusty's explosion, and I'll believe you if you swear to me that you didn't either. If you did get mad and lose your cool, you have to tell me. I can't protect you otherwise."

I jab my elbow into his gut. "We just had *incredible* sex. You can at least wait half an hour before you start being a jerk again."

His fingers dip under the sheet and splay across my stomach. "We don't have time for games and half-truths. We need to stay ahead of anything that comes for us. Other than wanting to know where I was, what else did Brown and Crybaby Luke ask you?"

I lace my fingers through Conner's. "You broke up Luke's marriage, so he's angry. That hardly makes him a crybaby. However, it does make me wonder if he would try to frame you for a crime. Could he be ticked off enough to rig that explosion? I mean, he could have done it thinking only the bar would burn or something, not with the intent to kill Rusty."

Conner's fingers twitch, tightening before loosening back into a relaxed state against my stomach. "I don't think he has the guts to try something like that. I think he's just looking for something to give him the satisfaction of arresting me. Which is how I know he's playing you. Up until you got here, he'd been fairly quiet about the whole affair. Abbie said he didn't want people to know why they separated. Now Luke is being free with the details. I think he's trying to set up a scenario where people will feel sorry for him. Probably so when he screws you over, he doesn't even have to come up with an excuse. Sympathy will already be on his side."

I scan his words for the line between truth and scorn. "I think the two of you are so embroiled in this battle over Abbie that you're not seeing each other clearly. Luke might be capitalizing on the situation, but when he explained his feelings for me, I believed him. I think he's being genuine. Partly, at least." I pull away from Conner's chest and glare at him over my shoulder. "Not because I'm flattering myself either. I have as long of a history with Luke as I have with you, it just happens to be of a different nature."

Conner cups his hand behind my head and pulls me to his mouth. "Yeah, and it's going to stay different because if you ever had any feelings for Luke, I would have known. Unlike you, I knew my partner. You'd throw doe eyes at Luke if I ever left you alone at a party, but the second I walked up, all you had was eyes for me. Those are facts, and he still can't stand that he's never beaten me at anything." Conner kisses me. Hard, like he's imprinting himself into my skin, claiming territory, and making sure to leave me wanting more.

I do.

I want all of Conner. Everything inside of me, places I didn't even know existed, scream for him. He breaks the kiss. "I'm not fighting for Abbie. I'm fighting for the same person I've been fighting for my whole life. You."

His words cut straight through me. I spin myself around and straddle his lap. His eyes gleam in satisfaction. I want to slap the arrogance off his face. Instead, I kiss him as hard and territorially as he just kissed me. "I can fight for myself. All I need from you is complete honesty. About things like you comparing Luke to his stepdad when everyone else says Luke is a great guy. If your ire toward him isn't about Abbie, it sure as heck isn't about me. So why are you against him? And how did the police so quickly conclude that Rusty's propane tank was tampered with? They never figured out the school fire was arson, and they've had more than eleven years to work on that case."

Conner lifts off the headboard and locks his hands on my hips, his face a solemn mask of the past, and I'm sure he's flipping through memories of the fire that demolished a large portion of our high school. "I was with you the night of the fire."

I squirm against his grip. "Yeah, I know. I'm not accusing you of setting the blaze."

He lifts one hand and circles my wrist, his other moving to cradle my backside so I can't get off his lap. "How do you know it was arson?"

I struggle to move. "You really are a piece of work, Conner Ferguson. I didn't set the school on fire any more than I set Rusty on fire."

He lets go of me. I scramble off his lap and away from the bed, snatching his pants from the floor and throwing them at him. He slides to the edge of the bed. "I'm not accusing you so stop overreacting and answer my question. *How* do you know the school fire was arson?"

I tug a t-shirt over my head and stomp to my nightstand, yanking B's diary from the pile of clothes and other books. I shove the diary into his face. "This is how, Conner. I found the arsonist's confession, and I've been trying to figure out who it is. I'll count you off my list of people who might want to help figure out if the author of this diary is still in Poca and blowing up lousy landlords!"

He flips the book open and begins to read, starting at the beginning the way I did. His face goes pale when he reads the entry about Kaity's car. I sit beside him. "What happened to Kaity Bell? Detective Brown asked me about her today. He said she left town when I did and that people were saying we ran off together."

Conner's hand shakes as he turns to the next entry.

August 12, 2012

I haven't been outside of the house for a while, so there's not much to write about today. My sisters are boring. Being stuck inside with them is torture. All we do is fight. They say the arguing is my fault, which is true. But they wouldn't have to hear me complain if they didn't have me grounded after my Fourth of July blowout. It was only a little fun. Who cares about Kaity Bell's stupid car anyway? I don't. Do you?

Speaking of cars... Watching them swerve around Sierra's drunk mother is the most fun I've had in over a month. She's passed out down the street. I can see her body lying in the road from my bedroom window. I hope Conner doesn't come along and drag her home. If she gets hit, I win the bet I made with my sisters. If he saves her, I lose, and I don't like to lose.

Don't worry, I'll stack the odds in my favor. Even if I have to run over Wanda Clifton myself.

Searching for the light...but you're scared to take a look.

B.

My breath catches at the sight of my mom's name. The threat. Conner shoves the book aside and gets to his feet, yanking his pants on without bothering to button them. I follow his movement through the room. "Where are you going? Do you know who B is?"

He snatches his shirt off the floor and tugs it over his head, throwing open the door and crossing the threshold. I chase after him. "Conner! If you know who B is, you have to tell me. My mother's *name* is in their book and I think they left the diary here for me to find."

He stops at the top of the stairs, looking back at me like he's lost every friend he's ever had. "Stay inside, Sierra. I have lawns to mow when the sun comes up, and I'll be back once I'm done. Don't leave the house. Don't take your mom anywhere. And don't talk to *anyone*. Especially Luke."

I stare at the space he was just in until his truck tires hit the pavement and squeal away. From the sound of the pinging metal as he pulled from the gravel drive, my rental probably now has dents in it. Worse than him running out on me and damaging my car is that Conner knows who B is, and from the glint of tears in his eyes, it's someone he's close to. Someone he's going to protect. "Someone he's choosing over me," I whisper to myself, hoping saying the words out loud will keep my heart from shattering. I always knew this day would come. Right at this moment, I'm not so sure it hasn't always been here. Conner talks a big game and he certainly delivers when it comes to the action, but once again, as soon he gets what needs from me, he's out of my bed and leaving me to deal with the rest of my life on my own.

I lift my chin and go back into my room. I don't have time to worry about Conner and his friends. I have a whole list of things to do around here today. Starting with stripping these sheets and ending with finally telling Mom that her alcohol dealer is dead.

~ *21* ~

Mom thinks I'm lying about Rusty's death so I can put her into a nursing home. I'm not sure how she's coming to that conclusion, but now that she's brought up the option of a nursing home, I am considering that as a possibility. Her brain scan is scheduled for the day after next. If the results confirm dementia, I'll start looking into homes that deal with that sort of thing. Tucking her away someplace safe just might be what's best for both of us.

I have no idea what's going to happen with the rental agreement Mom verbally agreed to. Only Rusty and she know what was really discussed, and if he went through the details of his verbal agreement with any of his family members, they could lie about the terms. I'd have no way to confirm. Wanda isn't trustworthy, and from experience, I know she'll spin things in her favor every single time she gets the chance. With the amount of work this house needs, I imagine whoever inherits it isn't going to feel very lucky. They'll have to make repairs in order to keep renting it, so whether they fix it up or tear it down, this dump is going to cost them. I need to keep that in mind as I prepare for the worst-case scenario. Which is currently comprised of getting kicked out of this house with a dementia patient in tow.

I check the pot roast, placing the lid to the crock pot back overtop the meal that will be ready in a few hours. Another scenario I don't have the energy for is Mom *not* getting kicked out of this house but ending up with a new landlord who is just as inept as Rusty. Technically, there's no reason for her to stay in Poca. I could take her to Dallas and resume my old life. A two-bedroom apartment shouldn't cost too much more than what I was paying before, and the little money Mom receives each month will help with the extra expense. What it won't cover is hiring a nurse to sit with her while I'm working.

If Mom does have dementia and I don't place her in a home, I'll eventually have to hire someone to stay with her because I have to go back to work. Especially now that I have whole extra person to care for. I'm not sure what a live-in nurse would cost, but maybe hiring one of those would be best. Then I'll have to pay for a three-bedroom apartment. Or a house. Neither of these will come cheap in Dallas. Homes there are quadruple what the same type of house would cost in Poca. Then, if I buy a house, there will be extra expenses such as lawn care and the general maintenance required of home ownership, like making sure the roof doesn't cave in. Buying a house also ties you to a location. While I like Dallas, what I love most is being free. As I proved when I came back to Poca, I could pack up and leave at any time.

I rub at the ache in my head and grab my bag from the counter, pulling out my phone. I have no doubt Mom will battle me tooth and nail if I try to force her out of this house and into a new one states away. The fight will be worth it, though, even if I have to tap all of my savings to cover moving expenses and down payments. The pressure of being in Poca is suffocating. Conner has singlehandedly seen to that. It isn't only him, though. It's B and Luke. I'm good enough to be dragged into drama and used, but not worthy of anyone sparing me enough time to even send an emoji. Once again, everyone is out living their best lives while I'm sitting around being a good little girl so as not to rock any boats. Well, Conner and Luke can both jump overboard and they can take their good buddy B right down into the depths with them. I'm tired of all of them.

I put my phone away and slip the bag over my shoulder, picking up a tray of assorted crackers I put together for Mom. I've stayed inside this house all day, exactly the way Conner asked, but I need groceries for tomorrow and he'd know that if he bothered to come back here the way he said he would. Or if he'd take the time to pick up his phone and check in with the girl he spent the night professing to love. I rekindled every single feeling I said I wouldn't, and this is what I have to show for it. Nothing but regret and bitterness.

I carry the tray into the mold room and place it on the small round table beside Mom. "These are peanut butter, cheese, and plain saltines. I'm going to the store. Anything special you'd like?"

She knocks over her empty can of ginger ale. "A bottle of Jack. I'm not drinking this garbage anymore."

I pick up the can and place it beside the fresh one sitting on her cracker tray. "I'm not Diana and Rusty is dead, so you drink soda, water, or nothing. Unless you want to start drinking tea or juice?" I raise a brow and wait for her to answer. "I can grab lemonade at the store."

She hacks up phlegm but I'm already backing away. "If you don't stop spitting on me, I'm going to muzzle you. Then you'll look like Hannibal Lecter, and still be drinking ginger ale."

I leave before she can say or do anything else. The grocery store isn't far away but maybe by the time I get back, her attitude will have shifted. I might even try to get her to play a game of cards. Anything to break up the boredom she has to be feeling. I'm more of a homebody than not, and even I'm going stir crazy in this house. Or, considering I slept with Conner last night, maybe the mold in here is just making me plain crazy.

I lock up the house behind me and inspect the side of my car for gravel-slinging damage, rounding the back and kneeling down to look at a mark etched into the paint just below the trunk latch. It's small and could have been here before Conner spun out of the driveway, but I prefer to blame him anyway. I smooth my finger over it, the mark ironically looking like a K, as if I need yet another reminder that Kaity Bell Edwards is the only missing girl this town wanted back.

I straighten and walk to the front of the car, sliding into the driver's seat. On top of my bad decision to sleep with Conner, I also made the very bad choice of not taking out insurance on this rental. That's going to cost me. The guy at the kiosk warned me specifically about rock damage, stating that he sees a lot of broken windshields. I didn't take his warning under advisement. In fairness, I'm not taking Conner's either. If he thinks I'm in danger from his buddy B, he should be sending the police after them right now, not ordering me to stay inside this house.

I back out of the driveway and head for the supermarket. So far, I've paid for all of Mom's food because if I try to use the government assistance she gets, she accuses me of stealing from her. When I speak to Aunt Diana next, I'm going to ask if she's willing to trade cash for Mom's food card. The alternative is bringing Mom to the store and praying she doesn't flip out in public when I force her to buy actual food. It's her unpredictability that keeps me from even considering buying a house that I can set up shop in, having clients come to me instead of the other way around. I'm not loaded, though. I can make do in Poca while living in Mom's mold-infested monstrosity, but if I move us, paying rent without an income will quickly deplete what I have to live on.

I turn into the parking lot of Poca's overpriced and understocked grocery store. Outside of a good deal of anonymity that comes with living in a larger city, another thing I miss about Dallas is food selection. I've gone from having virtually anything I want at my fingertips, to being scrutinized for selecting the organic version of the three egg choices in the store. Whether that scrutiny is good or bad depends on exactly who is eyeing the contents of my shopping basket. If the beehive of hair I can see over by the box of watermelons on the sidewalk is who I think it is, nothing I select today will be above reproach.

~

Mrs. Satter's disapproving stare is the same today as it always was. When I was growing up, she used to make her eight children stand on the corner at the entrance to the trailer park every Saturday. They were ordered to shove gospel tracts into the hands of anyone who happened by. If you didn't stop to take what the kids were offering or waved them off because you simply didn't want yet more paper to be wasted, Mrs. Satter would chastise you. Age or gender didn't matter to her, she was equal opportunity in her sanctimony.

She looks down her nose at me, pious as ever, and I feel the scrutiny scratching over my choice of a sweatshirt atop what she would consider underwear instead of shorts. I give her a polite smile, hoping my point is clear. I don't care what she thinks about my attire, and that includes my ratty flip-flops. She hands her credit card to the cashier, running her condemning eye over my attire again. "Where did you say you came from?"

I tilt my head. "Do you not remember me, Mrs. Satter? I'm Wanda's daughter. I came from the trailer court."

She turns back to Gina, the cashier who also happens to be an old classmate of mine. A cheerleader-adjacent one. She wasn't on the team but was always with them. "No wonder."

I roll my eyes. "You're right. You never brought your kids *into* the court, so you shouldn't remember me. God only cares about people who have money to fill the offering plate."

Mrs. Satter's mouth drops open, a severe glint turning to stone in her glare. She snatches her card from Gina's hand and grabs her two bags of groceries from the end of the register, storming off without another word. Gina snickers. "Good for you. No one ever talks back to her."

I place my basket onto the belt of the register. "At least we now know that she *can* walk fast with that stick up her backside."

Gina giggles again, looking me over. "Cute hair. It was really pretty when it was long, though. Why'd you cut it?"

I'm surprised she even remembers me, let alone how I wore my hair. She was in deep with the Ignore Sierra Club. "Not too long after I left Poca. It's easier like this." Especially when you never know when you're going to shower next.

"Hmm," is her only response, her hands working slowly to scan my items. "Mr. Duncan used to complain about the Satters to Mrs. Jeffries during gym class every day."

I laugh. "You're right, I forgot about the way Duncan and Jeffries used to sneak around like all the kids wouldn't figure out that they were having an affair."

She leans toward me conspiratorially. "Mrs. Jeffries and her family moved out of town three years ago, right around the time when Mr. Duncan was getting divorced."

I shrug and hand her my credit card. "Secrets never stay secret for long."

She prints my receipt and tucks it behind my card before handing it back to me. "For your sake, you better hope that's not true."

I put my card away. "What's that supposed to mean?"

Her nose crinkles, disgust turning up the edge of her lip. "What does what mean?" Then she whips her head around and greets the next customer with a cheery hello, chatting them up and making it clear I'm expected to move on. I grab my bags. I shouldn't be surprised that she's the same old mean girl she always was. Leopards don't change their spots.

I exit the store through the same set of sliding doors I entered through. I have no secrets that would matter to anyone in this town. At least not in a way that would change their opinion of me. I could give a sob story about being beaten when my mom was drunk, but the very fact that everyone knew she was a drunk should have been enough to garner any sympathy they had for me. There was only ridicule, and it spoke as loudly to me then as it is now.

I move through the fire lane at the front the store, pausing as a big gray truck with a camper top catches my eye. Conner's here. I scan the side of his truck and find him standing beside the hood, a heart-stopping smile on his face while his hand strokes the bulging belly of a woman whose long dark hair falls over her shoulders in waves of perfection.

It's shiny and thick, the kind of hair that tempts you to reach out and touch it, exactly the way Conner is right now. He sweeps it over her shoulder, softly touching her cheek before returning his hand to caress her stomach, the smile on his face matching the one I can now see on her profile. My gut flips. I don't know why I didn't consider it before, but Abbie isn't having her husband's baby. She's having Conner's.

A car horn blows and I jump. It's Mrs. Satter. She flicks a gospel tract out her window and continues past me. I look back to where Conner is standing with Abbie. They're both now watching me. Conner's head shakes, his eyes burning in warning. He doesn't want me to walk over there and cause a scene. As if I've ever done that to him. Conner has always been free to do whatever he wanted and I shouldn't let him get away with it this time, but I'm too embarrassed to march over there to tell the woman he's choosing that I'm so ignorant I let him lie his way into my bed last night. She's been having an affair so her personality is the same as Conner's. She won't care that I'm hurt any more than he does.

I leave the tract where it lies and march to my car, dropping the grocery bags into the floorboard behind the driver's seat before sliding behind the wheel. I don't waste time—I immediately start the car and shift into gear, pulling out of my spot. I catch movement out of the corner of my eye. Conner is now hugging Abbie, his arms wrapped sweetly around his pregnant mistress. I resist the urge to lay on my horn. I'm not road raging over to them, and I'm not driving by them like everything is fine either. I swing my car around and go the wrong way down the lane I'm in, looping around the parking lot and exiting on the far side. If I was petty like Conner, I'd drive over to the lovebirds and tell Abbie all the things he whispered to me last night. I'd give her the play-by-play and hope it caused doubt to seep into the dark recesses of her mind the way Mom's words always infected mine when she told me I was a joke to Conner. Doing that would only prove Mom was right, though. I won't give her *or* Conner that satisfaction.

<h1 style="text-align:center">~ 22 ~</h1>

I drive away from the supermarket, head pounding. My blood is rushing too quickly through my veins. I'm either going to be sick or pass out. The trailer court is up ahead, the decorative wooden fencing along the front entrance calling to me. I need air. And privacy. Both of which can be found in the patchy field of dirt and rock that lies behind the court. I turn through the entrance and pray nothing has changed as I wind my way through the trailers, finding what I'm looking for at the end of the paved road. I bump over the edge and keep driving, tires following along the rarely used dirt path that leads to the tracks. Thankfully, the railroad crew hasn't made it this far yet.

I grind to a halt at the end of the earthen access road. The trailers are behind me, the closest one tucked into the trees a hundred yards away. In front of me is the opening the railroad maintains in order to drive onto the tracks from here, just before the tracks begin to ascend up the mountain to where a train trestle spans the valley. I get out of my car and suck in a dusty breath, my powdery trail still billowing across the desolate field ahead of me. The breeze tosses my short locks forward, the ends tickling my chin and cheeks. Until I saw Abbie, I liked my hair. Now I know that Gina was insinuating my long hair was better, and it seems Conner would agree. He likes long and wavy locks. And Mom likes him. Since he's her new best friend, maybe his home is the one she should go to. I'm sure Abbie would love to have Wanda Clifton as a grandparent for their baby.

I wheeze in a deep breath. Burgundy strands of hair flash and frolic on the tracks ahead of me, whipping and wrapping, flying high into the air and far out behind the little girl who's watching me. I stare, frozen in place as the wind tangles and pulls at her. She was just outside Mom's kitchen window last night. If she's here now, does that mean she lives in the trailer court? With her parents? B? Is this trailer court B's connection to my mom? If so, it's how Conner knows B too.

I suck in another ragged breath and step forward. The little girl takes off, skipping over the tracks like they're as familiar to her as grass in her front yard. I run after her. I was never as fast as she is on the tracks, but I never tried to be. All I did up here was kill time.

"Stop!" I yell. She keeps going, rounding a bend by the time I even get to where she started. I kick off my flip-flops and push my legs into a dead sprint, pretending I'm on a sandy Texas beach instead of the rough-hewn wood and chunky, razor-edged rocks of the tracks.

I catch sight of the girl again but she's too fast, I'm still losing more ground than I'm gaining. She hits the part of the track that begins the ascent up the mountain and runs up the incline like *she's* the one on a beach. The increasing elevation isn't hampering her movements at all. Meanwhile, my lungs are burning and my legs are aching. Still, I keep going, hitting the incline and pushing my body as hard as possible.

The trestle is up ahead. I've never completely crossed it before. I've made it to the center and then turned back so I wouldn't have to walk the entire bridge just to return to this side. The valley below is deep and steep. Something you don't want to fall into or attempt to traverse. "Wait!" I try to yell, the sound more of a moan than a word.

Just before the trestle, the girl cuts down the embankment on the left, darting around the boulders and disappearing in the foliage. I slowly catch up, reaching the point of her disappearance. I bend over, resting my hands on my knees while I suck in air. I'm really out of shape. Or running is just a lot harder than I remember. "Come out of there." My yell comes out like the call of a dying goose. "I'm not going to hurt you. I want to know why you're watching me." I drag in three more breaths and then straighten, cupping my hands on my hips because I'm nowhere close to being recovered. "Who are your parents?"

The child doesn't answer. I move closer to the steep edge. "You're going to get hurt down there. Please, just come here. I'll take you home." Silence answers me. "I'll buy you an ice cream," I bribe.

Smartly, the girl doesn't fall for being offered candy by a stranger. I have to respect that. "Can you tell me your name and where you live? I'll send your family back for you." I wait, giving her time to consider her options. There's no sound at all up here. No birds, bugs, or little girls.

I climb onto the top of the nearest boulder and crawl to the edge, looking down into the valley below. "Are you hurt?" Still no answer. My fingers slide against something wet. I lift my palm. It's smeared with blue paint and glitter. I sit up and inspect my other palm. It's coated with the same fresh paint. My knee slides as I move. I look down at the hunk of rock beneath me. The whole surface is decorated with freshly glittered letter Ks. I scramble backward, feet and arms landing in splotch after splotch, paint and glitter crusting between my fingers and toes. I jump from the boulder, landing with a yelp on the gravel below. The wind kicks up. I swipe at the hair pelting my face, a sensation of wetness spattering across my cheek. I look around me. When I ran up here, I was so focused on the girl that I didn't notice her artwork. She hasn't only covered every inch of this one single boulder in paint, she's marked all of them.

I spin in a slow circle. All around me, brightly glittered Ks glisten in the sunlight. My thoughts snap to the mark on my trunk, the K etched into the frame of the mirror in my bathroom. This girl...she did all of it. Fear trickles through me, carving its way into my bones until it settles deep inside me, a coiled cobra biting and gnashing until my feet are once again moving. Running. This kid couldn't have known I'd be here today. Not when I didn't even know myself. She was up here alone, making a shrine for Kaity Bell Edwards.

My knees tremble. I flail my arms as I stumble back down the tracks, the sharp edges of rock slicing and rolling under my feet as I try to stay upright. My head is screaming that I just saw something I wasn't supposed to. Something railroad crews will soon stumble upon. I slam into a solid wall. No, not a wall, a man. My senses scramble and I pull away from him. He hauls me back to his chest, hands gripping my shoulders, shaking, words and sounds shouting from his lips as my heart hammers deafening blood through my ears. The diary, the kid, this man... I meet Conner's stormy eyes. He shakes me again, my name ripping from his frantic lips. "Sierra! Answer me. What were you doing up there?"

I latch onto his forearms, focusing on the solidness of his presence instead of the panic ravaging my nerves or the pain slicing through my feet. Tears burn my eyes. "She's up there."

Conner tugs at my sweatshirt, pulling my hands off his arms and flipping them over. He scans the paint covering my clothes and palms. "What did you do?"

I shake my head. "It was the girl. The one who broke into Mom's house...she's...watching me. She lured me... No, she..." Tears blob onto my cheeks. "The Ks...they're everywhere. All over the rocks. In my house. She keyed my car. They're everywhere. In glitter. Just like the ones the cheerleaders painted on their faces—"

"Shh," Conner dips into my face. "Calm down. Everything is okay now. Just go home." His eyes flit to the tracks behind me. "I'll take care of everything."

He releases me. I pull his shirt into my fist, words falling rapidly over my lips. "No. You can't go up there. The girl...what if she hurts you? What if she's B's daughter and B is up there with her?"

He grips my wrists. "Go home, Sierra. And this time, stay there like I told you to." He shoves me away from him. "Go straight home and when you get there, stay inside."

"No." I gape at him, reining in control of my senses. "You can't go up there. It's a trap. B is setting some kind of trap. We need to call the police."

He stomps toward me. "What you need to do is what I just told you to do."

I shake my head. "I don't care what B means to you, Conner. They're dangerous. Do you understand that? I think B might have hurt Kaity."

His body stills, cold eyes crawling over mine. "Shut your mouth and go home. Do *you* understand that, Sierra? Turn around, walk away, and forget you were ever here today." My mouth flops open but he shoots a hand forward, landing a fist in the air beside my head, teeth grinding. "Home. Now. Stay there until I come for you."

I back away from him. "What I'm going to do is find out who B is. You can't protect them. I'm going to find out who they are, and you better hope Abbie will give you an alibi for whatever it is that your precious B has done because once I have a name, I'm giving it to the police."

~*23*~

I stand in the cold spray of my shower, numb to its icy touch. I left the trailer court and came home, exactly like Conner ordered me to. I scrubbed my hands, carried in groceries, and served Mom her pot roast, sitting by her bedside afterward until she fell asleep. Thankfully she was docile when I arrived because these last hours have felt like I'm on autopilot, my body unable to do anything other than the bare minimum. I duck my head under the water and let it freeze me. There's so much conflict inside of me I can't hear myself think over the screams of indecision. After what happened at the police station the other day, maybe I've lost faith in them. Maybe it's only Luke I don't trust and that's why I didn't run straight to the police today. Maybe the real reason I didn't report the girl and her disturbing artwork is because of Conner's reactions to both the diary and finding me behind the trailer court today.

I turn off the water and step out of the shower, reflecting on how shaken I was when I saw the way those rocks glittered in the patches of sun filtering through the trees. It was creepy. Made worse by being in an isolated place where I doubt many people have ever walked. I was in that location with someone I've seen both outside and *inside* of my house. She's just a kid, and that makes the entire scene even more disturbing. Standing in that place laced more fear into me than I'm capable of processing.

I dry off and pull on a clean pair of sweatpants. In my haste to wash away the remnants of this day, I forgot a shirt. I walk bare-chested into my room and pull a warm sweater from the pile of laundry by my door. It's all clean, I just haven't had time to put it away. I dig through the pile for socks, not caring that they don't match. I'm probably going to end up bleeding all over them anyway.

I sit on the bed and inspect the painful cuts on my feet. Only a couple are particularly deep, the others just enough of a slice to draw blood. I did most of my bleeding inside the rental car, the paint drying but the blood keeping my feet slick as I worked the pedals and got myself back to this house as quickly as I could manage. I guess I shouldn't have ditched my flip-flops on the tracks. Maybe B or their little accomplice picked them up for me.

I take bandages from the ancient box I found in the back of a kitchen cupboard. The adhesive barely sticks but these will have to do until I can get out for some new ones tomorrow. I pull the socks on to help the bandages stay in place and take another painful walk right back out of my bedroom. I trudge down the stairs, a wince gritting my teeth together when the edge of the last step catches me right on one of the deep cuts. I keep walking, navigating to the back of the house and slowly opening Mom's bedroom door. As glad as I am that she was passive earlier, her subdued demeanor is now striking me as odd. She ate her dinner without saying a word, only speaking once I got her tucked into bed. She asked what my name was. Then asked what her name is. After I answered, she closed her eyes and was soon snoring.

Her door creaks as I close it, cutting off those now soft snores of her deep sleep. I move quietly into the kitchen and retrieve a roll of paper towels along with a bottle of white vinegar. This will clean the blood off the floor mat and pedals in my rental car. If there's any on the carpet, my spit will clean that. Mr. Reed, the drama teacher at Poca High School, used to tell the kids who were actors that if they bled on their costumes, they should spit on the blood and it would remove it from the garment. Apparently, it only works with the spit of the person whose blood it is. Which is why I never tried it out in that class. All I did that semester was clean the sets and keep the props organized. His spit trick is something I tested at home. Surprisingly, it worked.

I slip my sore feet into a pair of tennis shoes and quietly shut the front door behind me. I'll get a closer look at the scratch on my trunk in the morning. Tonight, all I want to do is clean the blood so there's one less thing for me to worry about when it comes time to return this car. I open the driver's door and flip on the dome lights. There's paint on the steering wheel. I rip off a paper towel and rub at it. I doubt there's much hope of cleaning all the glitter away, but most of the dried paint is flaking off, traces of it only remaining in the grooves of the textured wheel. I wet the towel with a touch of vinegar to see if that will clean the paint from the grooves. Red and blue lights flash on the roadway behind me. I duck out of the car and watch as Luke's cruiser pulls in, his high beams angling to blind me. I throw my arm up to cover my eyes. The high beams shut off, as do the red and blues. Luke exits his vehicle. "Sorry, I thought someone might be trying to steal your car."

I toss the paper towel onto the seat and straighten myself out of the way so I can close the door. I don't want to explain away the paint *or* the blood. "No, just me, doing a little cleaning since Mom is asleep already, and Poca is boring."

He walks around to the front of his vehicle and leans his hips against the hood. "I called you a while ago. Were you too bored to answer? Or are you planning on avoiding me?"

I take note of the clipped tone he's not entitled to and wave my hand with a sarcastic flurry. "I'm rarely graced with phone calls from Poca's fine residents, so I wasn't aware that I should even check my phone, let alone be glued to it. If you called because you're looking for Conner, as you can see, he isn't here."

Luke scans the yard as if he's making sure. "There's a lot going on lately and I'm still working double shifts, so I haven't been able to free up enough time to talk to you the way I want to."

I gird myself with resolve and rip the figurative Band-Aid off. "I slept with Conner last night."

Luke's body goes stiff but he doesn't say anything, he's only staring expectantly, like he's waiting to get the rest of the story. I wonder if this is how he reacted when he found out Abbie slept with Conner. I cross my arms over my chest. "It was a mistake, a spur-of-the-moment type thing. I'm only telling you about my bad decision because I promised to be honest with you. I also met your ex today. Well, I saw her at the supermarket. With Conner. She's ridiculously beautiful, so I get why you two are fighting over her, but I really need you both to leave me out of it because I also have a lot going on. Too much to worry about what lies you and Conner are telling just so you can each put one more feather in your cap. One that you're only plucking so you can later whip it out and wave it in the face of the other."

He sits there quietly for a while longer, finally showing signs of life by scrubbing both hands down his face. He blows out a long sigh. "Abbie is most certainly gorgeous. I felt lucky that a girl like that would want to be on my arm, and not only for her outward beauty. I wish I could say it was only skin deep but it isn't. Abbie has a lot of good in her. Those sweet and kind qualities are what made me fall so hard, so fast. I loved her. I still do, and I'm sure I always will. She's going to be the mother of my child. I'll give her the respect she deserves for that." He lifts off the hood of the car. "Abbie isn't perfect, though, and she, by far, is not the only attractive woman I've had the pleasure of knowing. So thank you for opening yourself up and laying all of that out for me. Honesty is what I respect most." He takes two steps toward me. "Abbie had her chance. She chose to cheat on me, so I ended that relationship. I won't be lied to. I guess that's why I'm not driving away from you right now. I don't have to like your actions to respect you for being a good enough person to speak the truth about them. That's the kind of foundation I'm looking to build on with someone."

I unfold my arms. "I'm not trying to lay foundations. I just want to be left alone. I think I'll be leaving soon anyway. I'm going to finish with the tests and doctors' appointments Mom has scheduled, and then I'm going to move us."

"Out of Poca?" he asks.

I nod. "There's not a single reason for either of us to stay within the confines of Poca." His face falls and I shrug. "I'm not you, Luke. Conner and Abbie didn't even have an affair behind my back, yet I'm still livid with both of them. I'm angry with you, too. And so tired of being strung along and confused by the actions of men who very clearly don't care what effect they're having on me."

He takes another step forward, close enough now for his hand to cup my cheek. "Trust me, I have a lot of hate floating around inside of me and enough confusion to make a spinning top dizzy. If you don't see my struggle, it's because I'm trying really hard not to hold anyone accountable for things that aren't their fault. You in particular. The second Conner approached us at Talico Bar, I knew he was going to try to sway you to his side and that the history you have with him would work against me."

I snort. "Yeah, it's working against me too."

Luke's smile is sad. "Conner was definitely wrecked when you disappeared, but I assumed the two of you were in contact. I figured he wouldn't acknowledge your name because he didn't want to rat you out. Now that I know you left without even saying goodbye to him, I understand the change his personality underwent. He wasn't only lovesick, he was ticked. Which has pretty much been his baseline ever since." Luke drops his hand from my face. "Conner's the last person I want to make excuses for but if he ends up being my son's stepdad, I need to be able to see him as something other than a backstabbing lowlife."

A laugh bubbles out of me and I slap a hand over my mouth. Luke playfully rolls his eyes. "Let me hear it. Tell me about how you women prefer jerks like him over *nice* guys like me."

Despite how he's trying to hide it, the hurt in his voice rings through, tearing at the strings trapping my heart in a nest of love for the boy who was Conner. "When a jerk turns on the charm, the change in personality is such a shock that we're in bed with them before our brains have time to catch onto the ruse."

Luke's chest rumbles in a deep laugh. "That must suck."

I nod. "It most definitely does."

He looks up at the night sky. "My emotions have been chewed up and spit out from underneath Conner's lawnmower, so I get that you're feeling as done with all of this as I am. But would you like to take a drive? I could use some company. Even if we're only sitting silently, it would just be nice not to be alone for a little while."

~24~

Panic is riding the waves of nausea swirling in my gut. "Can you hurry?" I ask Luke. "Mom can't be left alone like this. Not overnight."

He speeds up. "I'm sorry I fell asleep."

I look out the side window and wipe at the tear running down my face. I took Luke up on his offer for a drive and we ended up down at the river, watching the stars reflect off the water until we were both comfortable enough to start talking about nothing in particular. He asked about my life in Dallas and if that's where I thought I'd go back to when I leave Poca. From there, my memory is fuzzy. So fuzzy I don't know how I got into the backseat of his cruiser, but that's where I woke up. My clothes feel intact and my feet are the only things in pain, two facts that are doing nothing to tamp down the fear of having been drugged. Conner comparing Luke to his stepdad is all I can think of. It can't be true, though. This can *not* have happened to me.

The cruiser pulls into the driveway. I open the door before Luke has time to stop. "Whoa!" he yells. "I'm sure your mom is fine, but give me a second to park and I'll go in with you to check."

I keep moving, feeling better with my feet on the ground outside of his vehicle. "You said you're running late for work, so get out of here. I'll take care of my mom." I sling the door shut and race away from the vehicle, praying he doesn't come after me. I head for the porch, relief flooding my chest as I hear the sound of his vehicle pulling back out of the gravel drive. I scamper up the steps. My foot catches on the top board and I trip forward, my momentum carrying me stumbling headfirst into the siding. My knee jams into the doorframe and I come to a stop. I steady myself on the offending frame and drag in a breath. I'm lucky my head didn't hit a rotten spot and go completely through the wall.

I move to stand but just above my hand, etched deeply into the wood framing the door, is a freshly scratched K. I fight my lungs, gasping for the air they're trying to expel. "Mom!" I shout, regaining my footing and bursting through the unlocked front door. "Mom!" I race down the hall. She isn't in her room. I turn around and run back the way I came, catching sight of her sitting at the kitchen table, her head dipped and her hands folded on the table in front of her. I rush to her side. "Are you okay?"

Her head turns, pools of tears in her eyes. "I need a drink. Please. Just one drink."

I hug her to me and press a kiss to her temple. "I think I need one too."

~

Spackle. Paint. Car cleaning kit. While Mom is undergoing the brain scans Dr. Sparks ordered, I sit in the hospital waiting room making a list of what I need to purchase. I'm not going to buy much because I have no intention of making repairs to Mom's house. I just want to cover up the vile Ks that are being scratched into the wood. I also want to forget that I woke up in Luke's car this morning. I took inventory of my body and I don't feel violated, but I still can't explain why I was curled up with him in the backseat. I didn't have a drop of alcohol. All I had was a few sips from the bottle of water we both shared.

I wipe the thoughts of Luke away and once again focus on what I can control. Dr. Sparks said it will be a couple of days before he or one of his nurses calls with the results of today's scans. Once I have those, I'll know what kind of apartment to look for in Dallas. My best option is to go back to the life it took me so long to build. At least a portion of my clients should take me back, and hopefully, Becky will still have a booth I can rent. From there, I can deal with whatever care these tests say Mom needs. If she has to go into a home, I'll find one in Dallas. Whatever it takes, I'll make things work because that's what I've always done. I figure out the way forward and I do what I have to do.

"Miss Clifton?" A redheaded nurse I met earlier steps into the doorway that leads out into the hall. She's the one who brought me to this waiting room after I met with the hospital's patient liaison. Dr. Sparks advised me to go ahead and put the medical power of attorney in place and the liaison helped facilitate that process.

I stand. "Yes, ma'am."

She smiles. "Your mom is ready. She was a little upset after we administered the dye so the doctor ordered a sedative. She's awake and calm, and we already have her in a wheelchair. We'll help you get her into your vehicle and once you get home, she should be fine. A little groggy still, but fine."

I follow her out of the room. "Thank you for looking after my mom."

The woman nods sympathetically. "I can see in your eyes that you're about as scared as your mom was earlier. I've been there. My own mother had a brain tumor so I've gone through a similar experience. Whenever I'm dealing with patients and families, I try to remember how important doctors and nurses were to me back then. Sometimes, all we need is for someone to show us they care."

Her words stick with me. All the way back to Mom's house. In its simplest form, my one desire is to be cared about. Not showered with gifts or deeds, but just to have a single person truly care about my well-being. I want someone to care whether or not I smiled today. To ask how my day was and actually care about the answer. Maybe Mom will eventually be that person because something is changing in her personality. She's reverting into an almost childlike mentality, a softness coming with the change that is much better than having my arms clawed open. Only, the change she's undergoing is happening too fast. I guess it's possible that this is her true nature and it really was the alcohol that made her mean. With the liquor out of her system, maybe she's simply becoming the person she's always been. If that's true, my mom is a weak, scared little girl.

I tuck the blankets of her bed around her shoulders. Since we've been home from the hospital, she's cried four times. She never says why but when I hold her, the sobs rip themselves from her chest, exhausting her until she falls asleep in my arms. It's such a strange feeling to hold her like that. She's had a long day, though. Going inside the MRI machine scared her and if I was in her position, I'd probably feel the same. I press a kiss to her cheek and then cross the room, slowly shutting the door whose hinges I need to oil so they'll stop creaking. I pace to the kitchen to retrieve a jar of coconut oil. It's as good of a lube as any. I'm sure it will work magic on the rusty old hinges.

"Hey," a male voice rumbles, followed by a thunk.

I scream and spin around. Conner holds up his hands, a crumpled black duffle bag at his feet. "It's just me."

I throw the jar of coconut oil at him. The jerk catches it. I march toward him and take a swing but the jerk catches that too. Tears slam into my eyes and I grit my teeth. "Get out."

He tosses the jar down onto the top of his bag and releases me with a little shove to get me out of his personal space. He rubs at his eyes. They're bloodshot and swollen. "I'm not going to take this crap from you, Sierra. The past two days have been..." His shoulders slump. "I just need a little peace. Can you calm down and just sit with me? Or lie down with me? I need a nap that will last about three weeks."

I balk at him. "Me calm down? Because *you* don't want to deal with *my* crap? You lie to me, sleep with me, and then disappear so you can run back to your little pregnant mistress. What did you tell her, Conner? Huh? What did you tell your buddy B? I hope you told all of them to leave me alone and warned B that I'm coming for them just as hard as they're coming for me."

His head tilts to the side. "Sierra?"

I rip his black duffle off the floor and sling it. "Don't say my name like that. You are not going to patronize me. I'm not in the wrong here, you are. Get out."

He drags in a breath and stalks to where I threw his bag. He picks it up and unzips the top, pulling out his toothbrush. "I've been busy. Not because I was with anyone else. I haven't been here because I had things to take care of. For *us*. And we've never really talked on the phone, so I didn't call or..." He tosses the duffle back onto the floor. "I packed an overnight bag so I can stay here with you. I sold some things so we can take off when we need to. Whatever happens, wherever *we* go, I'm ready for it now. After all these years, I'm ready for *us*."

I stomp past him, grabbing my purse and digging out my keys. He follows me to the front door. "Where are you going?"

"If you won't leave, I will." I slam the door in his face. He yanks it open, hot on my heels. I march to my car. "Mom's had a rough day. If she wakes up, she'll probably be crying. Good luck with that. I'll be back to make her dinner, but there won't be any extra for you, so do *not* feel free to make yourself at home."

~ 25 ~

Conner has more nerve than a man ought to be allowed to have. He didn't only follow me from Mom's house and park his truck directly beside my car in the hardware store lot, but he followed me inside the store and now his hulking frame is lurking behind me. I'm doing my best to ignore his presence but it's impossible. I reach for a tub of what claims to be fast-drying wood spackle. He reaches over my shoulder and plucks the tub right out of my fingers. "What do you need this for?"

I face him, retrieving the item from his grip. "None of your business."

He frowns. "There's no point in fixing anything in that house. I already talked to Rusty's nephew. He's the one it was left to, and he doesn't have the money to fix it. He plans on trying to sell the house but said you and your mom can stay there until all the legal paperwork is settled, and his mom is contesting Rusty's will, so that could take some time."

I stare at him. "I mean what I'm about to say with the utmost offense, Conner. I don't believe you. Give me the name of this nephew and I'll talk to him myself." Conner's head shakes and I smirk. "That's what I thought. You like to keep the names of your friends close to the vest. I'll find Rusty's nephew, though, just like I'll find B. Your special buddy has messed with me for the very last time."

I step left but Conner slams his hands onto my shoulders, holding me in place. "What are you talking about? *B* did something to you? To hurt you?"

I drop the tub of spackle into the shopping basket dangling from my arm. "You read the diary for yourself. Then there are the Ks painted everywhere I look, and even scratched into my car. Didn't you see the brand new one on Mom's doorframe when you barged in again today?"

His hands slowly move away from my shoulders. "No, my mind was a little preoccupied."

"Yeah, well, it's clear that Kaity was your buddy's target, and I find it really strange that B is now targeting me. Were you cheating on me with Kaity *and* B? Others too? Did everyone know but me?"

He traces a thumb along my cheek. "I didn't fool around with other girls. I was yours alone, and *that's* what everyone knew. I'm loyal to you, Sierra. Even now, after all that you've done."

I point at my chest. "Me? After all that I've done? You're right, Conner. I should have stayed here in Poca because even though I was miserable, you were happy. And my mom? Heck, she wouldn't be as incapacitated as she is because I'm sure if I stayed here and kept letting her use me as her punching bag, she would have eventually decided it was more of a high to hit me than the bottle. I bet she would have gone sober, and I bet you still would have slept with another man's wife. Maybe I could be having your baby, too. In a shared room with Abbie. Wouldn't that be convenient for you? Both of us right there in the same room so you wouldn't even have to walk down the hospital hall to see all of your women or your kids."

He folds his arms. "That kid isn't mine, and you shouting about it in the middle of this store isn't going make the lie you're telling come true. *Your* buddy didn't make his wife happy, and *you* didn't make me happy, so two sad people had an affair. And yeah, I would have been happy if you didn't screw everything up for us. Me being happy doesn't mean you getting a raw deal, though. You were going to be out from under your mom's roof, and I was going to be with you. I told you that so many times. We only had to make it to graduation. Then we were off to wherever I had the best scholarship option."

I make a face at him. "Once again, I was to go where you went. Do what you wanted. What did you think was going to happen? I was going to hide in the closet of your dorm room all day and wait for you to take me out and play with me at night?"

He pulls his arms free and runs a hand down his tired face. "We talked about this, Sierra. You didn't plan on college so you were going to work, and we were going to find an off-campus apartment to at least rent a room in." He scans my face. "I didn't know you weren't happy with me. Half of our plans came from *your* mouth, and I loved you so much that I wanted all of it. Everything *you* said we would have and do. Then you blindsided me, and all I can think of now is that I saw your mom backhand you too many times to ever care about her as much as you do. Yet what's important to you is as important to me today as it always was. So I should have been taking care of your mom this whole time. I *would* have if I knew me not taking care of her would cause you to come back here."

I resist the urge to attempt slapping him again. "Do you think about your words before you say them? Or do you just let things spill out and hope your pretty face will cover up the stupidity?"

He doesn't respond. I move down the aisle. "First, he hates the sight of me and tells me to leave. Then he suddenly loves me and wants to sleep with me. Afterward, he ghosts me for two days. Now he's here pretending to care again, as if I don't know that before dinnertime, he'll be back to singing his original tune and ordering me to get out of his sight. Heck, he's already so adamant about not wanting me here that he wishes to rewind time so he can take care of a drunk, undoing the very reason for me to have ever shown up back in Poca."

"Sierra—"

I glare at him. "Stop following me, and stop saying my name."

He slides his arm around me. "I'm saying your name because I want there to be no doubt in your head that it's you I want, Sierra."

I throw his arm off me. "Did you even come to Dallas? Or was that whole lie part of the ruse to prove to both of us that I'm an easy lay?"

He grabs my hand and pulls me to him, his eyes tracing my features. "Not a single thing about you is easy. I want to try to help with that, though. I want to figure out how to make you see yourself the way that I do because I want the girl I had the other night, Sierra. She felt like she came back here for me, not for someone who abused her." He sighs and presses a hand to his heart. "I looked for you, but you never looked back. That hurts. Still, I'm here, and I'm doing my best to navigate this situation. I'm sorry if what I'm doing isn't good enough for you, but I'm standing inside this store with no privacy to have a personal conversation with you, telling you and anyone who's listening that I love you and only you. I have *always* been all in with you. *Always*."

I bite my lip, attempting to make myself bleed so his words will stop bleeding into my soul. "I don't believe you, and I don't trust you."

He slowly threads our fingers together. "Same. I don't trust you, and who the hell knows if anything you've ever said to me is true. I *want* to believe you, though. I *want* to trust you, and I want to figure out what it will take to have you trust me." He presses a kiss to my forehead. "I'm going to order us some takeout from the place next door. After we finish whatever errands you have, we'll go home and start talking through everything that's been going on the last few days. We need to be on the same page so we can come up with a game plan because I'm not asking you if you love me. I know you do. I felt it the other night, and I know I gave that right back to you, so let's just stop with all the nonsense and get ourselves together because there just might be light at the end of our tunnel if we work with one another and not against each other." He smiles down at me. "You want us back together as much as I do, so let's go for it. Let's see the world the way we said we would."

~

Conner's words don't alleviate the pressure of the questions I have over his behavior. Especially where B is concerned. He might have walked the entire hardware store with me, holding my hand and being unabashedly affectionate, but even when he insisted on paying for my purchase I didn't swell with comfort. I let him pay because I didn't want to cause a scene. I won't be the only person to connect the dots and think Abbie's baby is Conner's. For all I know, everyone inside that hardware store today already did the math and in their eyes, I'm just as pathetically in the middle of Conner's relationship with Abbie as Jan accused me of being with Luke. All the polite librarian did was attach the miraculous healing attributes of Abbie's kid to the wrong man.

If Conner wants to prove the baby isn't his, he'll have to get a paternity test. At this point, I doubt his word will hold any more weight with the people in this town than it does with me. Luke is no better, and I wouldn't trust Abbie's word either. Not that I plan on being here long enough to care what anyone in their triangle does or says. I'll be gone from Poca soon, and Conner can talk all he wants but it doesn't matter that he's right about me stupidly loving him, he isn't coming with me.

I pay for the two bags of food Conner ordered from Sam's Bistro and head back toward the front of the restaurant. I'm grateful that I don't have to cook tonight but since Conner paid at the hardware store, I insisted on buying the food. If I'd known how much he ordered, I would have made a scene inside the hardware store. That bill was a lot less than the one I just footed. I spin sideways and push the door open with my shoulder, one hefty paper sack dangling from each hand. Conner is waiting by our vehicles because I told him to and for once, he actually complied with what I wanted instead of demanding I do as he says.

I yelp as arms catch me around the waist and my feet go airborne. Luke chuckles, his lips covering mine before he sets me on my feet again. "If I get any happier to see you I'm bound to make you spill all that food, and it looks like it'll take a month's salary to pay for it. Treating your mom to a special dinner tonight?"

I stumble away from him. "What are you doing?"

His forehead creases. "Are you okay?"

I shake my head. "No, I'm not remotely okay." I look around us, keeping my eyes from the one place they want to go. I don't need Conner running over here throwing fists. "I woke up in the backseat of your car, Luke. *Nothing* about that is okay."

He chuckles. "I didn't think so either but after you started kissing me last night, I couldn't do anything other than just follow your lead. You are a *very* good leader, Sierra."

My mouth falls open. "I kissed you?"

The smile fades from his face and he steps toward me. "What's wrong? You're looking at me right now like I—"

"Drugged me," I slice.

He jerks as if I slapped him. "What?" A truck horn blows. One long, steady beat until Luke swipes his angry face away from mine and looks over his shoulder. Conner revs his engine and sticks his hand out the window, flipping Luke off. The cop turns back around and stares at me. "So that's what this is. You're with him, and you said and did all that stuff last night to set me up. For what, Sierra? He already has my wife and I'm humiliated everywhere I go by the whispers and the stares, people talking about the man who was dumb enough to sit around not noticing that his wife was screwing one of his best friends. What more does Conner want? My job? Is he running me out of town? What is the end game here? Because only over my dead and cold body will you get to make accusations like the one you just spewed. I didn't do anything with you last night except for what *you* initiated."

I shake my head vehemently and Luke yanks his phone from his pocket, pulling up a photo and shoving it into my face. "Do you look drugged? Because you sure as hell look fine to me."

I scan the picture. We're in the back of his cruiser. I'm sitting on his lap and have my head resting alongside his, a seductive pout on my lips. He flips to the next picture, where I'm nibbling on his ear and looking into the camera with sex in my eyes while Luke is blushing and sheepish. He pulls the phone away from me and stuffs it back into his pocket. "I thought it was weird that you kept wanting to take pictures, that's part of why I stopped you when you put your hand down my pants. I'm sure glad I was smart enough to pump your brakes. Take that straight to the hospital and get yourself a rape kit because my tongue was in your mouth and my hand got more than one feel of your breasts but no part of me was inserted into any part of you. Make sure you tell your boyfriend that. Real men know how to keep their flies zipped."

~ *26* ~

I'm trying to concentrate on the road but the images Luke showed me keep flipping through my mind. It was my face. My hair. But I don't pucker up for pictures and I've never been sultry. There was a confident glint in the eye of the girl in those pictures. She was sexy, and she knew it. Only a drunk or drugged version of me would ever do things like that, and I most certainly wasn't drinking.

I turn into Mom's driveway and take a breath. After Luke stormed away from me, Conner pulled out of the parking lot and I assumed he was heading here but his truck is nowhere to be found. Typical. It's probably better this way, though. I'm shaken to my very core and he'd only make it worse.

I carry the bags of food to the house, eyeing the K that will soon be patched and painted over. I wiggle my key in the lock and feel unease crawl through me as the door creeps open. I push it open farther and try being as quiet as Conner has been when he breaks in. Something in the air feels wrong. I might catch the little girl in here again, or I might catch B.

I move slowly, watching where I step and scanning every shadow. I reach the threshold of the mold room and look inside. "Mom?" She's sitting in her chair, the flickering light of the portable DVD player casting her movements in broken strobes. Her torso is still but her hands are moving. I walk toward her. Her hand comes up six inches, dropping back to her palm, driving the sharp tip of a metal fingernail file into her meaty flesh. I drop the bags and rush forward, grabbing her right hand just as it lifts again. The palm of her left hand is gnarled and bleeding, like rats have chewed and gnawed into it. There's blood spilled across her lap, down her legs, and onto the floor below. Bile rises in my throat and I yank the file out of her hand, throwing it across the room. "What have you done?"

She doesn't respond. Her face is blank, her stare unfocused, and her mouth making no sound at all. "Mom!" I scream, shaking her shoulders. "Snap out of it! Please. Mom, you're scaring me."

Footsteps pound into the room behind me. Conner drags me away from her, spinning me around to look at him. He speaks calmly. "Get a towel to wrap her hand and meet me outside. Got it?" I nod, still standing in place. He mumbles a curse and rips off his shirt, turning away from me and kneeling down in front of Mom. He wraps the shirt around her bleeding hand and then lifts her from the chair, cradling her in his arms like a child. He carries her toward me, reaching a hand from underneath her to wrap around my arm. "Sierra, honey, you're both in shock, but I need you to come with me. Okay, baby? I've got you. Just hold onto me, listen to my voice, and walk out to the truck with me."

~

I throw the last of the food haul from Sam's Bistro into the trash, the whole meal ruined in the hours between when I first dropped it and when Conner dropped me off back here after Mom was moved from the emergency room to a psychiatric floor in the hospital. I traipse to the door and pick up the flowers Conner dropped in the entryway earlier. I walk them back to the kitchen and set them on the counter. While feeding us from a hospital vending machine outside the emergency room, he apologized for not following me home. He was bothered by the way Luke greeted me with a kiss and instead of jumping out of his truck in a rage, he decided to do something he thought I would actually appreciate.

Growing up without money, Conner was never able to buy me flowers before. He'd pick dandelions and other wild growing things, but I couldn't afford to buy him gifts either so we mainly avoided the general awkwardness of gift-giving expectations. When other girls would do things on his birthday, like bake him cupcakes, he'd thank them but give away their gifts, saying he thought it was lame to be celebrated for something his parents did. That I know of, the only things he kept were the cards I made him and the gifts his family gave him.

On my birthday, there was nothing to keep except for Conner's neatly written letter. Even before we were officially dating, he'd write a full-page, front and back letter to me and leave it under my pillow the night before. After I left Poca, I would still get up on the morning of my birthday and check for his letter. Instead of cake and candles, checking for Conner's letter is my tradition.

I wipe a tear from my cheek. Just like back then, I have no idea what I would have done without him today. He took control of the situation when I couldn't. He got Mom to the emergency room and helped explain what he knows of Mom's mental state to the doctors and nurses. Because of that, Dr. Sparks was consulted and Mom was admitted for observation.

"Hey," Conner whispers as he enters the kitchen.

I turn away from the beautiful flowers and look at him. He glances from my face to the flowers and then slides the two large pizza boxes from his arm to the counter. "This all the food we can get this late. You still like onions and extra pepperoni?"

I nod. "Thanks. For the food, the flowers, being here..."

He rubs a hand over the grass-stained shirt he pulled from the back of his truck after Mom was safely inside the hospital. "No problem. I want to be here for you, so thank you for letting me." He grabs paper towels and stacks them on top of the pizza. "It looks like you've cleaned everything up already so let's take these boxes upstairs. We both need to sleep and I'm pretty sure we're going to crash before we even finish chewing."

I fumble with a glass as if my fingers are all thumbs. "You go ahead. I want to purge the house of all sharp objects. I'm going to replace the glass with plastic and lock the kitchen knives in my car or something. If she would have used one of those..."

Conner stills my hands, placing one of his over both of mine while his other rubs up and down my back. "We'll get everything figured out and taken care of in the morning. Right now, you need food and sleep."

He guides me away from the counter, bringing the pizza boxes and paper towels with us. I let him lead me up the stairs and down the hall to my room. Neither of us bothers changing. We crawl straight into bed. He rests the pizza boxes between us, stacking them with one edge on each of our touching legs. He flips the lid of the top one open and I smile at the offering. He always eats mushrooms and cheese on his pizza and on the rare occasion when he had enough money to buy us pizza, he always got half for me and half for him. "There are two pizzas. You could have ordered one for each of us."

He settles lower against the headboard and dives into his first slice. "I started to, but it felt wrong. This is us. Two halves of the same whole."

I lift a slice of my own from our whole and pick at the pepperoni. "I don't know if I deserved your help today, but I really do appreciate you staying with me tonight. Especially after I told you to get lost earlier."

He fits his arm around my shoulders. "I told you to get lost, too. Neither of us is great at listening. Not to what the other says or to what their actions are telling us. That's why I wasn't there for you the way you needed me to be back when we were kids. I tried, but I had so much going on with sports and trying to keep my grades up so I could get a scholarship that I just didn't get the message that you were in crisis. You weren't spelling it out for me so I missed it. I'm not going to do that again. We're getting a second chance and I promise I'm going to do better."

I shake my head. "We're not getting a second chance. Closure maybe, but even that feels shaky. I do love you and there are so many reminders of why, especially today, but..."

His arm tightens around me. "We're complicated, Sierra. We should both walk away from one another but instead, I'm going to try for a second chance because all the time we spent together as kids meant something to me. The days, the nights, and everything in between. You were never all I had, but you were all I ever wanted."

~

Conner's phone is ringing. I kick him. He doesn't move, his snore unbreaking as he lies beside me with his arm resting heavily around my waist. The ringing stops. I close my eyes, exhaustion dragging me back into a dreamland. The phone rings again. Stops. Then rings again. Whoever is calling isn't even taking the time to leave him a message. I flop his heavy arm off of me and sit up. "Conner." He's out cold. I grip his shoulder and shake. "Wake up and answer your phone or I'm going to throw it out the window."

The arm I just threw off of me stretches out, a groan on his lips as he slaps at the nightstand without opening his eyes. He lifts the phone and I catch the name on the screen as he swipes across it, still without opening his eyes. "What?"

"Conner!" Abbie's voice squeals out of the speaker.

He springs upright, clicking her off speaker and pressing the phone to his ear. "What? No, I'm not at home. I'm with Sierra." His face goes slack. "What body?" His wide eyes snap to mine, terror crawling out of them and slithering all over me. I tug the sheet up to my throat as if that will calm the squirming mass of unease. Conner gets out of bed. "I don't know. I'll run over there and check it out. Thanks for calling." He hangs up and yanks his shirt from the floor beside the bed, pacing the length of the room and back again before meeting my eyes, no less terrified now than he was before. "Railroad crews found a body buried under the tracks behind the trailer court."

A sharp inhale nearly drags my tongue down my throat. I cough. "When? Who?"

He sits on the bed, his eyes brimming with tears. "Kaity Bell Edwards."

"What?" I whisper.

He sniffs. "I didn't know they were going to reach the trestle this soon. I watched the progress for most of the last two days…"

"The trestle?" I shake my head to stop the bombardment of thoughts. "Where B's little girl marked the rocks? Why would you be watching the railroad's progress?"

He cups my hand in his sweaty palm. "Look at me, Sierra. I need you to concentrate. Okay?" I nod and he exhales. "Good girl. Just stay focused because I have to go. I'll be back as soon as I can but while I'm gone, I need you to pack. Do you understand?"

I shake my head. "Pack for what? You're scaring me, Conner."

He pulls me closer. "You don't need to be afraid. Just pack, and I'll be back here before you know it." He kisses me. Before I can protest he's off the bed and running out of the room. A shudder rips through me. The downstairs front door slams behind him. His truck starts up and he guns the engine, once again kicking up gravel as he spins out of Mom's driveway and squeals onto the road. I sit shivering on the now cold bed. If he was watching the tracks, he knew Kaity's body was under them.

~*27*~

The sterile smell of the hospital is making my already upset stomach feel even worse. Mom has been sleeping most of the time I've been here, the same as she is now. I slip out of her room and walk down the hall to the bank of elevators. I need fresh air. The doors ding open and I step inside, followed by two nurses. I hit the button for the lobby and step to the back where I'll be out of their way. "How do they know it's Kaity Bell?" the dark-haired nurse asks over the squeak of her crisp white shoes. "Didn't they just find her body right before nightfall?"

The short nurse with hair cut similar to mine tugs on a chain that's around her neck. "The necklace. Kaity's mom gave her that diamond-studded K for her sixteenth birthday. There was always suspicion that if she met with foul play, the necklace would show up in a pawn shop. Well, it was foul play alright, but that necklace was right there, still around the poor girl's neck."

Bile crawls up the back of my throat, more than it did when I was staring at Mom's ripped and torn skin. I press myself farther into the back of the elevator. The nurse with the squeaky shoes shifts her weight, her head shaking. "I just can't believe it. She was so young, her whole life ahead of her. Who would do such a thing?"

The second nurse snorts. "Probably the person who knocked her up. Yolanda's brother is on the railroad crew and he told her that when they uncovered the skeleton, right there in the center of all the bones was a perfectly formed skeleton baby."

I gasp right along with the second nurse. They both turn to look at me as if they're just now realizing someone entered the elevator ahead of them. The doors ping open and the women get out. I stay where I am. There was a day in the lunchroom when Kaity and Conner were playing footsie under the table. They'd both been laughing and I felt too awkward to walk across the cafeteria and sit down next to him while that was going on, so I stayed on my side of the room and sat at a table by myself. Ten minutes later, Conner seemed to finally notice I wasn't there. He stood up and started looking around the room. I slipped out of my seat and through a side exit before he could find me sitting there staring at Kaity and him. I was used to the flirting but if I could avoid being present for it, I did. I assumed when Conner finally chose someone else, he'd dump me. I didn't know he'd sleep around, get a girl pregnant, and then kill her.

The elevator doors open again and I rush out, chasing hallways and doors, looking for a way out. A sign over the stairwell says exit. I shove through the door and race down the steps. Luke was wrong. Conner was never wrecked because I left. He was destroyed because he killed Kaity Bell and their unborn child.

~

I bolt through the doors of the police station praying Luke is here. I can't say this to anyone else, confess to what I know about Conner, his involvement with Kaity, and his recent behavior. I place my palms flat on the front counter. "Is Sergeant Putnam here? I need to speak to him. It's urgent."

The female officer rests her hand on mine. "I can see that you're upset, and I'll call Putnam for you, but why don't you tell me what's going on first?"

Tears pool in my eyes. "I can't. I really need to speak to Luke. Please. Tell him Sierra Clifton has something important to tell him, and it can't wait."

She pats my hand. "Have a seat and I'll see if I can reach him."

I sit on the wooden bench positioned on the wall across from the desk. My head and heart are hurting, not to mention my feet and all the rest of me. I glance at the clock on the wall above the desk. I've been here five minutes and already it feels like hours.

I sit quietly and replay every word Conner said to me this morning. Every word the nurses spoke. Finally, the door opens and Luke stomps in, fire in his eyes. He marches directly over to me and leans down. "If you're in here spouting that crap—"

I grab his shirt, my frantic words barely escaping my constricted lungs. "Conner killed Kaity."

Every muscle in Luke's body freezes. His eyes look between mine, searching for truth, lies, what my angle for saying this could be. Tears spill over my lashes. "I'm sorry for what I said to you yesterday. I don't know what's happening to me. I haven't felt right since I came back here and..." I let go of him and lower my head. "I don't remember any of what you have photographic proof of, and it isn't the first time I've lost chunks of time. I'm scared. What if..." My throat bobs. "Conner has a key to my mom's house."

Luke wraps his hand around my arm and tugs me to my feet. "Come with me."

I do as he says, tears dripping down my face. He leads me past the room I was in before, through the stares of other officers and personnel, and into a blank-walled room smaller than the cushy interrogation room I was in last time. He pulls a plastic chair away from the wall, its metal legs scratching over the tile floor. "Sit."

I do. "Maybe Conner is the one who drugged me. He might have put something in my food..."

Luke pulls another chair out for himself and places it right in front of me. He sits down and leans forward. "If he did, we'll figure it out." He cups my hands in his. "Don't be scared. Just start over, from the beginning, and tell me everything. Don't leave anything out, because you've now made two serious accusations in as many days, and I just came from the morgue where I had to see one of my good friends rotted away to nothing but bone." His hands tighten on mine. "Take a breath, and then slowly tell me every single thing you know."

~

Consider us even. Luke's last words to me ring over and over, the satisfied glint in his eyes eating at something deep inside of me. I didn't tell him about the diary, still possessively protective of its contents, but he didn't need that information to put a case against Conner together in his mind. He listened to everything else I said, hanging on my every word. Words he's going to use to hang Conner with. Now that I've said them, I wish I could take them back. I can't, though. Maybe that's why B left the diary to begin with. They wanted me suspicious of Conner, so I'd know that their secrets aren't the only ones buried in Poca.

I walk into Mom's empty house. Luke suggested that I stay at the hotel in town since Conner has been walking in and out of this place with ease. I stare down the hall to the back of the house where the kitchen is. Where flowers are on the counter and possibly tainted food is in the cabinets. Nothing about being drugged by Conner makes sense but I don't plan to even take my toothpaste with me because I can't account for the oddity of my own behavior any more than I can reconcile the boy I knew with one who would kill his pregnant mistress.

Concern for Abbie fills me as I slowly walk up the stairs. I imagine Conner turned on Kaity because at that stage of his life, he thought a child would ruin his plans of going on to play sports in college and beyond. That baby would have tied him to Kaity, at least financially. With money having always been a hard thing for us to come by, supporting a child would have felt beyond the realm of possibility. So he permanently removed his obligation. Only, B knew what he did.

I pause at the top of the steps. What if Conner was B's boyfriend? The one who went on the acid trip that ended with Kaity's car disappearing. Maybe B hated me as much as Kaity because I was another one of Conner's bimbos. Maybe B *is* a male, and that's why Conner never coupled up with him publicly. They might have been teammates, hooking up under everyone's noses, while Conner made B feel the same way that I did. Convenient. What if it was me who got pregnant instead of Kaity?

I shudder against the darkness of my thoughts, forcing my legs to walk despite the hollowness inside of me. I turn into my room and freeze. Conner is sitting on the bed, his face expressionless. "You didn't pack like I told you to."

I back out of the room. "Where's your truck?"

He gets off the bed and stalks toward me. "I ditched it. Your car is better on gas so we're leaving in it."

I angle down the hall and slowly keep backing away from him. "I'm not going anywhere with you."

The corner of his mouth turns up, his eyes growing hard and the muscles in his arms jumping. "Why not?"

I reach the stairs and grasp the rail. "Kaity is dead."

His steady pace brings him closer. "I know."

I step backward, fumbling to get my footing on the first step. "She was pregnant."

His eyes widen a fraction, showing his surprise that this information has spread so soon. "I know that, too."

I pull my left foot down to join my right one on the step. "Because you're the father."

He growls, his whole face contorting in disgust. "Luke's stepdad is the father."

I lose my footing as I try for the next step. Conner lunges forward, yanking me back up the stairs and spinning me into the wall. He presses his finger into the center of my forehead. "You. I only slept with you. Ever. Until Abbie. Get that through your thick head, Sierra."

My body goes numb, knees weak and throat dry. I want to believe him but... "You didn't sleep with her, but you killed her? For Luke's stepdad?"

His nostrils flare. "I didn't kill her."

I look into his eyes. "Then who did?" His jaw ticks, but he doesn't answer. He keeps staring into my eyes, the hardness softening as he does. I gasp. "This is why you always told me to stay away from Gerald Putnam. It's why you wanted me to stay away from Luke, isn't it? You think Luke knows what his stepdad was doing with Kaity, which means he must know what Gerald did to her. You're worried they're going to pin the murder on you and use me to do it."

He releases me and I slide down the wall. "That's why you never left Poca. You've been guarding Kaity's body so Gerald couldn't...move her? Implicate you?"

Tears swell in his eyes. He looks up at the ceiling. Sirens roar outside and he snaps his eyes back to mine. "What did you do?"

I wrap a hand over my mouth, tears rushing down my face and over my knuckles. I shake my head and Conner shouts, punching the wall over my head. His chest heaves and his teeth grind, words fighting to stay in his mouth as the sound of tires squeal to a halt outside. He shoves away from me and disappears behind the thick sheet of plastic covering the door to the spare bedroom. Fists pound on the door downstairs, Luke's voice loud as he calls my name and demands I open the door. I stay where I am. The pounding stops and footsteps fill the downstairs, more shouts reaching their way up the stairs to fill my ears. I stare at the plastic. A body fills my view and a warm hand cups my cheek. "Sierra," Luke speaks softly. "Where is he?" I keep my hand pressed tightly over my mouth. Luke shifts closer. "Conner sold his truck for half of what it was worth and I know he pocketed that cash and came for you. He's going to run, and we need to stop him. Do you understand?" I nod. Luke smiles all too easily. "Okay, now tell me where he's hiding because I know he's here."

~ *28* ~

I stare out the window of my hotel room, the single-story building serving weary travelers who happen this way, not-as-discreet-as-they-think hookups by the hour, and those kicked out of their homes with no place else to go. I fall into the latter category. Luke and the men with him scoured every inch of Mom's house. They didn't find Conner but the mold damage and rotten wood in the room I last saw him enter was enough for Luke to call the house uninhabitable. I obviously don't disagree with the assessment, but I scrubbed and bleached everything I could.

I close the curtain and go back to the bed I barely slept on last night. I packed Mom's clothes into a trash bag and left it in the back of my car along with her DVD player. My suitcase is in the room with me but I didn't bother retrieving more than my toiletries and the clean pile of clothes I never got around to putting away. Luke didn't say I was never allowed to go back inside the house, only that the place needed to be condemned. In light of that, I was once again reminded that I very well could be suffering from the effects of mold inhalation. Which explains my odd behavior much better than the idea of Conner drugging my toothpaste.

I sit gingerly on the edge of the bed. Obviously another reason Luke wanted me out of Mom's house is because he has the place under surveillance. He fully expected Conner to be there and since he wasn't found and I denied seeing him, the expectation of Conner appearing there will continue to inform Luke's decisions. I wish I had such clarity. All of my decisions are being informed by a cacophony of disagreeing voices. Conner being a murderer felt wrong from the start and most of the voices agree with that assessment. The dissent comes when I try to process how he got involved with knowing the location of Kaity's dead body. He might have caught Gerald in the act of dumping Kaity's body and the man made a threat against Conner's own life. Gerald might have forced Conner to help him. Gerald could also have nothing to do with it. Whatever happened, Kaity Bell Edwards was never missing. Conner knew exactly where she was and he never told anyone.

My phone rings. I pick it up, unsurprised to see Luke's name on the screen. He called twice last night. He says it's to check in to see how I'm holding up but it's really only to know if Conner has reached out to me. I made this whole thing so easy for Luke. That night at Talico Bar, he told me what Gerald used to do to a mentally challenged woman while Luke complicity distracted the woman's son. I should have run then. Instead, I ignored all of Conner's warnings and played straight into Luke's hands. I answer his call. "Hello."

"Hey." Luke's tone is reserved. "Can you come down to the station?"

My chest tightens. I don't want to go anywhere near Luke again but I got Conner into this mess so it's my responsibility to get him out. "Sure. When?"

Luke doesn't hesitate. "Now."

~

I flip back through the stack of nondescript postcards that represent the past eleven years. They're postmarked from all over the country, each signed with my name, though only a handful of them are in writing even remotely close to my own. "I thought you said you didn't communicate with Conner after you left?" Luke asks from his seat in the cushy interrogation room. I feel Detective Brown's eyes watching my reaction to the postcards just as intensely as Luke is.

I smooth my fingers over the embossed maple leaf on the front of a card that was postmarked in Maine four years ago. The back simply reads. *Tastes like you on Sunday mornings. Love, Sierra.* My heart constricts at the words. Conner's mom ritually made his family pancakes on Sunday mornings. When I'd kiss him later, he still tasted like syrup. "I have no idea who sent these to him."

Luke pulls out another card, one with a yawning kitten on the front of it. He flips it over. *The slut needs cuddles. See you soon, baby. Love, Sierra.* It's postmarked from Colorado only two months ago. "Convenient, don't you think?" Luke accuses.

I pull my hands away from the cards that are all addressed to Conner at his old address and what I assume is his new one. "I didn't even know

Conner was still in Poca until I got back here, so no, it isn't *convenient*. Coincidental to my actual arrival here, maybe, but you can take my handwriting samples and my DNA right now. I didn't write or send any of these."

Detective Brown shifts forward. "Have any idea who did?"

I look at the pile of cards that Conner had grouped together by year. At least, Luke said that's how they were found when a search warrant was executed on Conner's trailer. "No. I think Conner knows, though, because the person is framing him for murder." I glance at Luke. "I was wrong. Conner didn't kill Kaity. He knows who did, though, and he hasn't been able to tell anyone about it."

"Why not?" Detective Brown draws my attention.

I swallow, not wanting to name Gerald in front of Luke. I'm not even sure I can trust the detective or anyone else in the police department. What if they decide that framing Conner is better than having one of their own arrested? "You'll have to ask Conner. All I know is that he didn't kill her."

Luke huffs out a laugh and leans back into his chair, folding his arms over his chest. "How did you come to this sudden change of heart? Just yesterday you were in here crying and telling me all about how Conner *did* kill her."

I lean away from the stack of postcards on the table and fire a shot in Luke's direction. "What I told you yesterday is that your wife called Conner yesterday morning, waking both of us up. She was upset over Kaity's body being found and when Conner ran off to go comfort her, I misinterpreted his actions. Did you have Abbie come look at these postcards? She's been in Conner's life the last eleven years, unlike me."

Luke's eyes narrow. "You can't protect him. Now that Kaity's body has been found there will be evidence that doesn't hang on the whims of a jealous ex-girlfriend. Rest assured that if you had anything to do with the murder, we're going to find that out too."

"Me?" I choke on my own spit.

Detective Brown taps the air with his hand, as if telling me to calm down. "It might be that you only knew Mr. Ferguson hurt Kaity. Maybe that's why you ran away. Whatever the case may be, we can't help you unless you tell us what you know."

"Help me?" I balk. "The only help I need revolves around my mom. The help Conner needs is a police department that isn't biased all because one of their officers has a straying wife." I shove the cards. "Look at what someone has been doing to Conner. Yeah, I messed up yesterday because I was spooked and misunderstanding things, but now you have proof that something bad is happening to Conner. *Help* him. Not me."

Detective Brown rubs at his jaw. "If he needs help, he needs to come in and speak with me. Can you get that message to him?"

I shake my head, not taking his bait. "I have no idea where he is. I haven't seen Conner since Abbie called him."

Luke grunts and Brown pats the air again, this time for Luke's benefit. "We all want the same thing, right? The person who murdered a little girl to be brought to justice."

I pan my eyes to Luke's. He certainly knew what his stepdad was doing with Heather, so he may very well know what Gerald was doing to Kaity. Willing participant or not, she was a kid. A beautiful, popular one. I highly doubt she *wanted* to have sex with a middle-aged cop.

A knock sounds on the door, breaking through the options I'm weighing in my head. It's hard to know how much or how little to say.

Thankfully, the person knocking doesn't wait to be invited in. A tall man in a suit just like Detective Brown's walks in. "Luke, you have a phone call." He looks to Brown. "I need to speak with you. Now."

Luke leaves the room without a word to anyone and Brown pushes out of his chair as if the movement is nearly too much for him. "Sit tight, I'll be back soon."

I do as instructed, resisting the urge to flip through the postcards again. I'm sure that's what they're expecting, all of them standing in another room watching the camera feed for signs that I'm hiding something. Maybe *not* flipping through the postcards is what makes me look guilty, as if I don't have to go through them again because I already know what each card says. I lean forward and rest my elbows on my knees, cupping my head in my hands. My skull is pounding. Being in this room is only making it worse.

I get up and pace around the room, trying to distract myself with thoughts that aren't centered around Conner. Mom was due for another psychiatric evaluation this morning. The results will dictate whether or not she can go home, home now being the hotel room. Whenever they release me from here, *if* they release me, I need to check in with the hospital. Before bringing Mom to the hotel, I'll need a fresh supply of bandages to keep her hand wrapped the way the hospital has it. They'll also have to give me instructions on how to treat the area because a few of the puncture wounds were too deep to bandage over. I suppose I'll need to follow up with Dr. Sparks again, too. His office hasn't called yet, but when they do, I'll see if they can recommend a doctor in Dallas.

I sit back down and slide the postcards to where I can look at the one on top without flipping through the whole stack. I'm sure I recognized B's handwriting on some of them. Did he or she have multiple people write the cards, telling them what to say and how to sign the cards in order for them to all bear my name but yet come from locations around the country? Why? Obviously, they're messing with Conner. They know intimate details about his life, but I assume Conner's mom making pancakes on Sunday wasn't a big secret. His brothers had girlfriends, and I'm sure those girls tasted the sweetness of syrup on the tongues of their Ferguson the same as I did mine. So is B one of those girls? Is B someone who was hurt by Gerald Putnam the same way Heather and Kaity were, and now they're hell-bent on torturing Conner because he was involved in covering up Kaity's murder? I look up at the camera in the corner of the room. Did Gerald Putnam receive postcards just like these?

I get up off the couch and pace the room once more. Surely Conner saw the differences in the handwriting and knew the cards weren't from me. He kept them to try to figure out who was sending them. I run my hands up through my hair and pull at the roots. No wonder Conner is so angry. He's spent eleven years being forced to wait for the day the world would finally finish collapsing around him, being reminded each month that the end was coming. B made sure the writing was on the wall.

I move to the door and crack it open. Detective Brown and the other man are standing five yards away, heads together. I catch bits and pieces of their whispered conversation. "...foam coming out of his mouth." ... "...poison..." ... "...lying on the bathroom floor..." My heart stops beating. I step out into the hallway, head swimming and vision blurring. Detective Brown's eyes snap to mine. "I'm almost finished here, Miss Clifton. Have a seat. I'll be with you shortly."

I shake my head, willing my nerves to be strong. If these men are talking about Conner, I can't stay here being forced to hear the rest. Forced to answer more questions while I'm dying inside. "I'm supposed to be at the hospital," I lie. "I have a meeting with my mother's doctor. I can come back when I'm done."

He draws in a breath and exchanges a look with the second man. One that says he knows I'm lying and he's trying to decide what he's going to do about it. I walk toward the two of them, what I hope is an easy and slightly cheery smile on my face. "I hate to leave like this but it can't be helped. I need to be there for my mom. I'll give Luke a call when I leave the hospital. Let him know, please." I follow up my words with another smile that I hope is polite and not creepy and walk right past them, keeping my feet steadily moving toward the front of the building. My body grows lighter with each step. So far, they're not stopping me.

I push out the exit and keep my pace even as I cross the lot to my car. Without looking around, I open the door and drop into the driver's seat. I blow out the breath I've been holding and start the engine, backing out of the parking spot and filling my lungs with air again as I navigate to the road. In case they're tailing me, I go where I told them I was heading. If Conner committed suicide, the hospital is the place I need to be anyway. If he's dead because of what I've done, my heart is going to explode.

~ 29 ~

I flip through the channels on the television in Mom's hospital room. She's awake but refuses to speak to me. I don't feel like talking, so that's fine by me. I scroll through the channels until I find the local news. The anchor's overly rouged cheeks frame the heavy makeup on her eyes, her lips downturned as she relays what I've spent the last couple of hours waiting to hear. "Yet another tragedy has struck our town," she begins. "Proving bad news does come in threes. This morning, Gerald Putnam, a former sergeant and beloved friend of so many in our small community, was found deceased in his home. No further details are available at this time."

Relief floods me. I tune out the rest of the broadcast. Surely Gerald Putnam is the foaming-at-the-mouth person Detective Brown and his cohort were talking about. Conner is still alive. I hope.

Gerald's death is timely, though. If he is the father of Kaity's baby, did fear force his hand and he took his own life? By poisoning himself? Considering my recent speculation about my own behavior, poison being used is chilling. "Miss Clifton?" A particularly short woman calls from the doorway of Mom's room. Her dark hair is pulled back into a severe knot at the nape of her neck and her hands are crossed in front of her.

"Yes?" I answer.

Her beady eyes dart to Mom and then land back on me with force. "I'm Dr. Andrick, your mother's attending psychiatrist. I need to speak with you."

I glance to where Mom is still focused straight ahead, not acknowledging the doctor's presence any more than my own. "I'll be back soon," I tell her, giving her arm a gentle rub before I leave her.

I follow Dr. Andrick down the hall and into a room with a small desk and mounds of paperwork. She points to a chair. "Have a seat."

I bite off the snippy retort forming on my tongue and do as she says. Dr. Andrick rounds the desk and tugs the squeaky faux leather wheeled chair around to where I'm seated. Neither of us says a word until she's sitting in front of me, her hands crossed over her lap in the same fashion as when she was standing in Mom's doorway. "I'm just going to get straight to it, Miss Clifton. Your mother informed me this morning that she did not mutilate her hand. She says *you* did."

The bottom drops out of my stomach. "Why on earth would she say something like that? Is it normal for dementia patients to lie about self harm?"

Her lips purse. "Your mother doesn't have dementia. I spoke to Dr. Sparks myself not even an hour ago. His initial assumptions were wrong."

I shake my head. "Then what's wrong with her? Why is she lashing out, forgetting things, and hurting herself?"

One of Dr. Andrick's fingers ticks against the back of her left hand, the rhythmic motion hypnotic. I look away from it and back to her face. "Well? Is it the alcohol withdrawal? I asked Dr. Sparks if I should let her drink some and he said no."

Dr. Andrick's finger stills. "There was alcohol in your mother's system when she was admitted. She says *you* gave it to her, and then proceeded to stab her in the hand for drinking it."

I stare at Dr. Andrick. "That's impossible. I cleared all of the alcohol out of the house as soon as I got there. There's no way my mom has been drinking under my watch. I pulled off every couch cushion and literally searched every nook and cranny. There's no alcohol left."

Dr. Andrick drags air in through her nose. "Miss Clifton, I have the blood reports. Your mother was drinking the night she was admitted."

"No."

"Yes." Dr. Andrick cuts me off before I can say anything else. "Are you abusing your mother?"

"Of course not!" I yelp. "I gave up everything to come back here for her."

"And did that make you angry?"

I get out of the chair. "Yes, it did. But not nearly as angry as you're making me. I did not give my mother alcohol, and I sure as heck didn't stab her in the hand with a nail file. I wasn't even home when she attacked herself."

Dr. Andrick motions to the chair, as if ordering me to sit back down. "Can anyone confirm that you weren't home?"

"Yes," I snap. "The hardware store, Sam's Bistro, Conner Ferguson, and Sergeant Luke Putnam. Now if you'll excuse me, I'm going to go speak to my mother and find out who brought her alcohol."

Dr. Andrick's seat creaks as she lifts out of it. I make it to the door before her words turn my blood to ice. "I've asked the hospital to deny you any further access to your mother until I can confirm the validity of her claim. You won't be allowed to see her again today."

Rage and frustration course through me in equal measure. I face her. "Not only am I seeing my mother, I'm removing her from the grounds. She'll be coming home with me. You can consider yourself dismissed, I'll find a psychiatrist who can actually help her, not one who's going to ignore what's written on the wall in front of her."

I turn back around and exit the room, storming back to Mom with angry words still fresh on my lips. I'm not sure what legal grounds I have here, but unless the cops are called, this hospital is not stopping me from removing my mother. I can only hope that dropping Luke's name will keep them from calling the police. I don't need more trouble than I already have and if the hospital happens to call Luke directly, I doubt he'll be thrilled about having to provide me with an alibi. He can either be honest with them and confirm what he knows of my timeline, or he can use Mom's allegation to haul me back into the interrogation room. At this point, there isn't a single thing in my life that doesn't feel like a toss-up.

I walk into Mom's room. Her eyes snap shut. I move to her bedside. "I know you're not sleeping, and I'm fine with you not speaking to me. All I need is for you to get up because you're being discharged. I'm taking you home."

~

Mom didn't say a word when I took her to the hotel instead of her house. I thought she would fight and fuss but it seems she no longer has the energy for that. I guess that's why I felt comfortable leaving her alone again. In her subdued manner, she sleeps a lot. There are also no sharp objects in the hotel room, and I asked the front desk clerk to let me know if anyone sees Wanda wandering about.

I walk out of Mom's house with yet another bag of dry goods from the pantry. There's a police car backed into the brush fifty yards away. Whoever is sitting inside of it didn't stop me from entering the house and, so far, they haven't stopped me from packing up bags and loading them into my car. I left my back door open in case they wanted to look through what I'm removing from the house. The only thing I don't want them to find is B's diary. I have it in the bottom of the bag I'm carrying now, flour and other pantry items piled on top of it.

I settle the bag onto the backseat with the rest of them and close the door, locking my car before heading back inside of the house. I leave the front door open, signaling that I won't be long and that I have nothing to hide in here. I walked through the whole place when I first got here. Conner isn't hiding out anywhere.

I stop at the kitchen counter and place two sandwich containers full of biscuits into a brown bag. I follow that up with a jar of peanut butter. Before I started packing, I took the time to make two batches of biscuits. They baked while I gathered the rest of what I wanted from this house. The second batch of twelve biscuits are wrapped and sitting on a platter that I'm taking to Luke. Usually when someone dies, it's appropriate to take food to their family and while biscuits aren't part of the typical fare, I'm hoping Luke will appreciate the gesture. Enough to open up about what happened to Gerald. I need to know how the man died. Poison or natural causes? Self-inflicted or murder? I also want to study Luke's reaction to his stepdad's death. It isn't lost on me that Luke seems to be in the middle of Rusty's murder, as well as Kaity's. His connection to Kaity might be negligible, but if he knew that Gerald was sleeping with her, Kaity's body being found could have made him confront his stepdad about the baby.

I fold the top of the brown bag down. It's still possible that Luke's water bottle was laced. He could have pretended to sip the way I was, but instead had only let the water tilt to the top of the bottle without drinking it. All I'm certain of is that if Conner is able to get back into the house, I want him to find this bag. I can't leave a note telling him the food is for him, but surely he'll peek inside and know I left it for him. If the cops find it before he does, I'll pretend I packed the food for myself and accidentally left it behind. "Please be safe," I whisper, running my fingers over the bag in hopes they'll imbue it with my words. In the complexity of what I feel for Conner, my heart breaks whenever I think of him alone and hungry, hiding. He might be gone from Poca now and I hope he is, but I don't know how a wanted man starts over. I had it easy. I already had a driver's license when I left and was able to obtain copies of my birth certificate by mail. Not being a fugitive and having no one looking for me, I was able to build a life for myself. Conner won't have that luxury.

I turn away from the counter and slide my house key onto the table. I won't be back. Ever. Neither will Mom. Whoever wants this place is welcome to it. I lift Luke's tray of biscuits from the table and head to the front of the house, sweeping out the door without so much as a backward glance. I should have done this the first day I stepped foot back in Poca. Left and never looked back.

~ 30 ~

I navigate across town to the row of townhouses Luke said he moved into. I'm not sure which unit is his, or if he'll be here or at his mom's house. Since his mom's place is a crime scene, I thought coming here was my best bet. Judging from the police presence and groups of civilians milling about the fourth home in the row, I'd say I made the right call.

I park in what looks like an overflow lot at the end of the row of homes and lift the tray of biscuits from the passenger seat. I get out of my car and walk toward the front of the townhouse. The bystanders watch me approach, judgment in the eyes of the few people whose stares I bother meeting. An officer shifts uncomfortably, as if he's contemplating stopping me from entering the house. I wonder why. Am I making these people uncomfortable because of my connection to Conner? Have they been told that I'm somehow involved in Kaity's murder? Rusty's? Gerald's too? Or has word of Mom's allegation spread beyond the walls of the hospital? I'm going to take another wild guess and say the suspicious looks I'm getting are due to some combination of all of the above. I need information, though, so I'm not going to wither under their scrutiny.

I waltz up to the front door, stepping aside as an older couple exits. Since the place is packed, I don't bother knocking or asking for entry. I slip through the door behind the exiting couple and wind through the pockets of people while scanning each room for Luke. My main reason for being here is to get information on how Gerald died but I also know all too well that even if a parent is evil, as their child, you still care about them. If Luke is grieving, I genuinely want to offer my condolences. If he's responsible for Gerald's death, maybe I'll recognize the falsity in Luke's grief. That alone will go a long way in corralling the many conflicting thoughts in my head. I need them all pointed in the same direction, or else I can't think straight.

The kitchen isn't hard to find. I head that way to add my offering in with the rest. The countertop bar that looks out into the living room is full so I go around it. Luke is in here, off to the right, in Abbie's arms. She's holding him and stroking the back of his neck gently as she coos softly into his ear. He tilts his head back and looks down into her face. A stab of betrayal shoots through my chest. Despite what he said, Jan was right about him. He loves Abbie and they're going to work things out. Not because of the baby, though. It looks like Gerald's death is the catalyst Jan was hoping for.

My eyes track down to Abbie's belly. One of Luke's hands is splayed over the side of it and his other is wrapped around his wife's back. He's holding her close, their eyes locked on one another as he absorbs the comfort she's offering. I suddenly feel like the interloper the accusing eyes outside claimed I was. I shove my biscuits onto the crowded island that's already nearly as full as the countertop and spin on my heel. Luke's throaty voice stops my retreat. "Sierra."

I turn back around, shoving all the sympathy I can muster into my expression. I tap the tray I brought. "I heard about your stepdad passing and wanted to offer my condolences. You have plenty of food so these can be frozen." I glance at Abbie since she'll probably be the lady of the house and taking care of this spread of food. "The biscuits reheat well. You can even put them back in the oven to warm them and they'll be fine."

Her small upturned nose wrinkles as she presses pause on the conversation she was having with her husband, her eyes embracing me warily. "Thank you. I'll pack them away with what's left of the others you made for Luke."

He smooths a kiss against her cheek, the same way he did to me a few times. "I'm going to walk Sierra out but I'll be right back. Go sit down, you don't need to be on your feet doing anything in this kitchen."

I start to wave him off. I don't need B to spell this situation out for me in their diary. I know when I'm not wanted. However, if there's a chance I can still get information about Gerald's death, I'm going to take it. Knowing Luke will follow, I turn away from Abbie and walk back out the way I came. I've never been formally introduced to her but she knows who I am just as much as I know who she is. Maybe even more. Conner casually told her he was with me, and that implies that he talked to her about me. Which is more than he or Luke ever did for me when it came to knowing about her. Conner said mostly nothing and Luke's descriptions of her were vague. The comment she just made was meant to carry weight, though. She's telling me that she's still a part of her husband's life.

I would explain to her that I don't want her husband but now isn't the time for such explanations. I can't even tell her that if she really wanted Luke, she wouldn't have screwed Conner. I'd rather let the two of them figure that out on their own because once a cheater, always a cheater.

It likewise isn't the right time to demand the baby's paternity be tested. Not that I have a right to demand such a thing at any time. The identity of the baby's father doesn't affect my life. I have no claim to Luke or Conner. But if the kid is Conner's, I really want to know.

Luke follows me to my car. I open the door to signal to everyone gathered here that the interloper is leaving. "I'm sorry to have barged in. I heard the report about Gerald's death on the news and wanted to do something to offer you my sympathy."

He nods. "I appreciate it."

His eyes tell a different story than his words do, but I'm not inclined to apologize for being catty when he had me locked in an interrogation room drilling me about postcards that I obviously didn't send to Conner. "What happened? Did Gerald have a heart attack? I never heard you mention him being sick, only that he retired."

Luke's eyes track between mine. "Looks like poison. Isn't that something? You bring up me drugging you, Conner drugging you, and now Gerald really did get drugged."

I shift my weight to lean against my car. "Are you saying Gerald overdosed? Or did he drink antifreeze?"

Luke's brows draw together. "Who said Gerald did anything to himself?"

I fold my arms. "No one. I guess I just assumed."

Luke wipes a hand over his mouth. "That's funny, because what I've been assuming is that my mom is in there grieving the death of her husband right now because Conner thought killing Gerald would draw attention away from Kaity being found."

My laugh is laced with incredulity. "Has anyone bothered to get DNA from Kaity's baby yet? If not, get it. Then compare it to your stepdaddy. I bet the results will make your mommy stop crying for the lousy, cheating, manipulative child rapist she married."

Luke's face turns red. "What did you just say?"

"You heard me," I snap, unfolding my arms and dropping into the driver's seat.

He leans down. "Yeah, I heard you. Now you hear this. Conner is sitting in my jail right now. He turned himself in not half an hour ago, and it won't be long before I turn his entire world upside down. You better hope you're not complicit in his deeds because if you are, I'm going to find the strings and pull on them until your whole world unravels right along with his."

~

I pace the sidewalk outside the hospital, chewing my nails. In the short time since I left Luke's townhouse, I've bit all of my nails right down to the quick. I don't know what he meant when he said Conner turned himself in. For what? Questioning since the police were looking for him? Or did Conner confess to murdering Kaity?

I spit another chunk of nail out of my mouth and pace back through the landscaping to the front entrance to the hospital. I called Aunt Diana as soon as Luke walked away from my car. She's not happy with my decision but in light of recent events, I need her to become Mom's medical power of attorney. Aunt Di is going to meet me here and Mom's patient liaison is going to redo the paperwork. In addition, Aunt Di is going to set the record straight on Mom's lies. Luke is clearly trying to rope me into everything he's tying Conner up in, and if Mom's allegation isn't rebutted, he has a ready-made reason to lock me up in his jail too.

The best solution for Mom is to assign her care to Aunt Di. We've already discussed putting Mom in whatever type of home Diana can find for her sister, and I've promised to send money each month to help with any associated expenses Mom's state aid won't cover. In the short term, Mom will go home with Aunt Di today. Once they're safely on their way out of Poca, I'm going to start knocking on doors and asking questions. I want to spread the word that Kaity's baby is Gerald's. That should buy Conner time. I only hope he was telling me the truth about the baby being Gerald's and not his. Same as I hope Abbie's baby isn't his. If Conner ever has a child, it should be with me. Every bone in my body and every voice in my head agrees with that. Conner is mine.

I scan the parking lot for Aunt Di's car. Since Kaity's body was discovered, more glittery Ks have popped up all over town. They're everywhere I look. On every light post and telephone pole, in every shop window, and even painted on the windows of cars in this parking lot. Kaity is all anyone is talking about. Every visitor, nurse, and outpatient who's walked past me has had Kaity's name on their lips. With Conner in jail, it won't be long before his name is whispered right next to hers.

A police car squeals into the parking lot, sirens and lights blaring. Another screeches in behind that one, followed by two more. I freeze. The cars slam to a halt in front of me. Doors fly open, people shout. I raise my hands, not sure if I should drop the phone I'm clutching or not. Uniformed officers swarm the sidewalk around me. Footsteps beat over the concrete behind me, closing in. I let go of my phone. It cracks against the sidewalk and skitters forward. Luke emerges from the back of the second cruiser, his booted foot crunching my phone under his sole. His eyes flick to mine. A nurse slams into my shoulder from behind. I keel left and an officer shoves me back the way I came. Another pushes me farther away, off into the shrubbery as two more nurses run past with a wheelchair between them.

I lower my hands. The commotion isn't about arresting me. It's over Abbie. The front of her black suede babydoll dress is matted and tears are streaking down her face. "It's too soon," she wails as Luke coaxes her from the back of the cruiser and into the wheelchair.

He races alongside her and the nurses as they hurry Abbie toward the doors. "It's okay," he tells Abbie. "The baby is going to be fine, honey. Our son is going to make it and so are you."

I step into a tall section of landscape, out of the view of the officers as some remain on the sidewalk and others go inside. The ones outside run fingers through their hair and hands down their faces. I listen intently as their disconnected words reach me, recounting the scene as each of them saw it unfold. Abbie first began to bleed, blood dripping from between her legs and splattering over Luke's living room floor. Before they got her into a police cruiser, her water broke and she began screaming.

"Stress…" I hear one of them say, and all I can think of is the amount of stress Conner is under right now. The police will rally around their own, as they just proved. Even if Gerald murdered Kaity and all Conner did was help cover it up, Conner will be held solely responsible for the murder. Not because Gerald is dead. Because Conner had an affair with Abbie. The woman who might be miscarrying his baby right now.

I move through the landscaping and go out the far side, walking away from where the officers are milling about. I ignore every glance in my direction and make eye contact with no one. I'm not even going to attempt to retrieve what's left of my phone. If so many officers are here, and some are still undoubtedly with Luke's mom, not many can be left at the jail. If there's any chance at all that I might get to speak to Conner, this is it.

~*31*~

I circle the police station parking lot and hope Aunt Di forgives me for not being there to meet her at the hospital. Conner's life is on the line and I want him to know that I'm not abandoning him this time. I want to look him in the eye and get the truth about what happened to Kaity and about who B is. Depending on what the truth is, B might have information that can exonerate Conner. Plus, I have a bargaining chip in the form of their diary. If they know Gerald killed Kaity and they'll give that information to the police, I won't tell anyone they set the high school on fire or stole Kaity's car.

I park and tug the bag holding B's diary into the front seat with me. I rifle through the flour and cans of peas, digging the book out of the bottom of the bag. If I do make this happen and I get to speak to Conner, I want to know what the rest of the diary entries say. I'm positive he knows who B is and if I have information that makes it seem like I do too, Conner might open up and tell me himself what actually happened.

I flip through the pages, picking up on benign entries full of nothing but complaints about never getting to go out and do anything fun. In one entry, my name appears, wondering about Conner's relationship with me. *Does he ever call you by the wrong name, little one?* The diary taunts, hitting the tender nerve inside that always kept me on edge, waiting for Conner to choose someone over me.

I flip to the last entry.

September 14, 2012

I should have drowned Kaity Bell when I sank her car to the bottom of the river. Not that it matters now. Bashing her over the head with a rock worked just as well. The tramp is gone. The only regret I have is Conner. If he hadn't been trying to find you, Sierra, he wouldn't have found me standing over Kaity's body. Then I wouldn't have had to force him to help me hide the tramp.

I gasp. Gerald Putnam didn't kill Kaity. Neither did Conner. B did. I shake my head, reading over the confession once again. Conner is involved in this because he was looking for me and stumbled across a murder. I check the date of the diary entry. September 14th is the night I left Poca. Conner was walking to my house while I was busy walking out of town. I glance at the police station. Did B kill Gerald because they know Gerald is the father of Kaity's baby and now that her body is recovered, B worried that Kaity told Gerald who her stalker was? It would make sense for him not to confront B after Kaity disappeared. The underage girl was pregnant with his child. He might have guessed that Kaity was dead and knew if her body was ever found, his involvement with her would come to light.

I'm now certain that B is the one who has spent these last eleven years taunting Conner. Just as certain as I am that they planted this diary for me to find. Not to warn me, but to taunt me too. Which I assume means that they've also been taunting Gerald in some way. The one person Conner, Gerald, and I have in common is Luke. Instead of me, it could have been Conner that Luke had a crush on. Some guys did, and Conner was aware. He treated those boys no differently than anyone else, and I can see how easy it would be to mistake his amorous nature. I was his girlfriend and mistook the way Conner interacted with other girls for something that it wasn't.

A memory floats to the forefront of my mind. The summer before senior year, I was at Conner's trailer when some of his teammates stopped by. Luke was among them, and Terrance, who wasn't on the team but routinely hung out with the others. The guys were teasing Terrance because apparently, he had a crush on Conner. So they brought him over to egg him on. Terrance shooed me away like I was a bug crawling on his man. Conner latched onto my hand and spun me into his arms, holding me tightly as he told Terrance, "If I wasn't straight as an arrow, I'd shoot myself straight into your pretty face. But I have Sierra's pretty face to look at every day and no one in this world has ever turned my head the way she does." The boys all laughed, taking his comment in a lewd way and proclaiming Conner liked my face because it gave him good head. Conner kicked them out, but it was Luke who was angry and shouting. Conner was sitting with me, asking if I was okay and apologizing for his idiot friends. Later, after everyone had left except for Luke, the three of us took a walk into the field behind the court. Luke picked a wildflower. He didn't hand it to me, he gave it to Conner, who braided the flower into my hair, claiming, "She's the only reason wildflowers grow in the trailer court. Otherwise, it would just be dusty and dirty, not a beautiful thing in it."

I close my eyes on the memory. There was never any malice in Conner, only kindness. I look back at the diary entry, B confessing without remorse to murdering Kaity and signing the page with a sentiment never truer than it is right now. *When you're searching for the light, sometimes you're too scared to take a look.*

I close the book and get out of the car, fear quickening my steps. No longer fear of the dark, but of the light. As scared as I am, I have to do this for Conner. The whole town is finally going to see the truth. Conner is not a murderer, and Gerald Putnam is not a hero to mourn. If Luke is B, he might have picked the letter because many people would call Kaity by her middle name Bell. Whatever the reason, if Luke and B are one and the same, I'll expose him. I march into the police station and face the same woman I saw when I made the mistake of thinking Conner was capable of murder. "Is Detective Brown here?"

Her facial expression says I'm the last person she wants to see today. "Would you like to tell me why you're looking for Detective Brown?"

I straighten. "Sure. Tell him I need to speak to him regarding Kaity Bell Edwards, Gerald Putnam, and Conner Ferguson. You can also tell him that I'd like to speak to him sooner rather than later, and that I'll be waiting for him in my usual room." I push past the counter, heart racing as I walk myself to the cushy interrogation room. Whatever happens, I refuse to walk out on Conner again.

~

I can't tell what Detective Brown is thinking. Or his cohort Detective Stanley for that matter. The taller man keeps glancing at me as Detective Brown reads through B's diary again. "Where did you say you found this?"

I sit forward on my seat, a little bit of a lie mixing into the truth. I can't very well tell them I've had it all along. "It was in a bag of stuff that I grabbed from my mom's house when I went back to clean out the kitchen cabinets and gather the rest of our things. I just found it a little while ago."

Detective Brown hands the book to his partner. "Let's get a full documentation done and see if the lab can pull anything off it."

Stanley nods and leaves the room. I chance asking Brown questions that I probably shouldn't. "Do you think you can get DNA off the book?"

He shrugs. "Maybe."

I swallow. "Has any DNA been found on Kaity's body?"

He studies me. "You say this book just fell into your lap, and you told me before that you're not involved with Conner Ferguson. At least one of those things isn't true."

I nod. "I am involved with Conner. I didn't know exactly how much when you asked about him before, so I wasn't lying. I figured we'd talk through the way I left him behind in this hellhole of a town, and then we'd be done. I was wrong. Being wrong about my feelings for him doesn't mean I'd fabricate a diary."

He clicks the top of his pen and scribbles something in his notebook. "Let's see here, your theory about Kaity's death is that someone forced Mr. Ferguson to hide the body, and he kept that secret for eleven years?"

I meet his cool stare with one of my own. "Conner didn't tell because whoever B is, they have a lot of pull in this town. Or *had*. You'll soon find out that Gerald Putnam is the father of underage Kaity's baby. Now Kaity, Gerald, and their child are dead. Which makes me wonder what Luke Putnam has been up to lately. I know for a fact that he was well aware of how his stepdad abused his position as a police officer. He's also one of the people who used to always call Kaity *Bell*. Maybe you should ask him if fabricating diaries goes hand in hand with fabricating postcards."

Detective Brown lifts from his seat. "Stay here, Miss Clifton. I mean it. Do not leave this room."

~*32*~

I hang my head, knee bouncing as I continue to wait in this sweaty room. I've been inside for so long I feel like I have a good idea what solitary confinement is like. The door finally swings open and I lift my head to suck in a draft of fresh new air. Conner shuffles in, rubbing his wrists. I jump off the couch and rush at him. He freezes, eyes wide and dripping with terror. "What are you doing here?"

I throw my arms around him. "I came for you."

He pushes me away and turns to Detective Brown. "Get her out of here. I don't want to see her. I already confessed so whatever she says is—"

"Shut up," Brown snaps. "One or both of you is lying." His eyes flit to mine. "Some of what you said is checking out though, so you get comfortable while I check on the paternity of the baby that's just now getting ready to enter this world."

He slams the door and I shudder. "They know Gerald is the father of Kaity's baby. You were right, Conner, and now the police know."

He fists his hands into my hair and pulls me to within an inch of his mouth. "Stop talking. This is what they want you to do. They put me in here with you so you'll give them everything they want. They're setting you up."

"No," I whisper. "They know you didn't kill Kaity. It's in B's diary, Conner. B confessed to bashing Kaity over the head and admitted that you stumbled upon the scene and they forced you to help hide the body."

His face goes slack. "B wrote about the murder?"

"Yes." A tear tracks down my face. "Tell them who B is. That's why they brought you in here, so that I could persuade you to let them know who killed Kaity."

He shakes his head, pulling me closer and looking into my eyes. "Valerie."

"What?" I ask. "The Valerie my mom talks to sometimes? That's who killed Kaity?"

Tears pool in his eyes. "Please, Valerie. You have to help her."

I smooth my hands along the back of his neck. "I will. I'll help Valerie. Just tell me how. Who is she, Conner?" His fists tighten. "Ow, you're hurting me."

He shakes his fists, teeth grinding as my hair rips from the roots. "Bobbi."

Tears streak down my face. "Stop, Conner. Please."

His grip loosens and he cups my face, tears streaming from his own eyes. "I'm sorry. I'm so sorry, Sierra, but you have to make them help you. You have to call for Bobbi. Please. She has to get you out of here."

"I...I don't understand."

He sniffs, pressing his forehead to mine. "I know you don't, Sierra. They do, though. Valerie, help her. Please. Show her. Let her see." He searches my eyes. "Valerie? Bobbi? Please, I'm begging you. Show her. Show her!"

Nausea floods my body, my vision in and out of focus as if my equilibrium is being pushed off center. Conner whispers Bobbi's name again and a barrier breaks open inside of me. I hear him screaming Bobbi's name. Not now, but in the past. On the night of Kaity's murder.

I back away from him, bumping into the table. His chest heaves. "Good girl. You see her now, don't you? You see them all."

My chest tightens, sweat breaking across my entire body. I shake my head, the present fading into the past, hazy outlines surging to the front of my consciousness. Me standing in the shadows watching Kaity Bell leave Conner's trailer. He walks her to the edge of his yard, wrapping her in a tight embrace and wiping her tears as he speaks to her softly. Another hug, his head resting atop hers the same way it rested on mine when he hugged me that way. He pulls away, cupping her face and pressing his lips squarely to the middle of her forehead.

I grab my chest, the pain inside of me today as raw as it was when it first exploded inside of me that September night. "You loved her..."

Conner closes the distance between us, keeping his voice low so no one else can hear. "No. She told me what Gerald did to her and I was going to help her." He wipes the tears from my face, not bothering with his own. "I love *you*. Even now. That's why I hid her body for you."

I cover my mouth, vomit rushing up my throat. I ran out of Poca in a haze of heartache after I flew into a rage, following Kaity from Conner's house and murdering her in cold blood. He stayed to make sure no one ever discovered what I did.

Sobs jerk out of me. Conner dips into my face. "Shh, not here, baby. You have to go." He pulls my hand from my mouth. "I'm sorry I didn't realize the others weren't a game you played until you got back here. I thought you were just having fun role playing." He presses his salty lips to mine. "Now it's too late for me, but they got you to safety before. Let them do it again. Go, Sierra. Run from this place and don't you ever come back."

He shoves away from me and I gulp in air, lungs tight and unwilling to expand. Conner opens the door. The little burgundy-haired girl is standing on the other side. No, not a girl. Me. Valerie. She crooks a finger, face serious as she darts down the hall. I push away from the table, lightheaded and unsure if anything I'm seeing is real. "What's wrong with me?"

"Nothing," Conner's voice breaks. "You're perfect. Now go. Please, I'm begging you."

I stumble into the hallway and look back at him. He begins to shut the door. "Forgive me, Sierra. I swear I didn't know they weren't you. If I did..." His head falls. "Please take care of my Sierra."

He shuts the door and I want to run at it, bang on it, claw my way back to him, but I can't. I have no control over my limbs. My feet move away from the door, shoulders straightening, and hands drying my tears. I scream but no sound leaves my lips. I exit the police station, closing in on my vehicle, knowing without looking that inside the trunk, there's paint and glitter. Images of me tagging the boulders around Kaity's body play like a reel before my eyes. I did all of it—the postcards, the etchings, the school fire. They're showing me all of it. My sisters. The personalities living inside me, rising up, screaming, yelling, begging me to see what their consciousness already knows. They can't contain Bobbi anymore. Not on their own. They need me, the original.

"But you're weak." Bobbi laughs, her voice coming out of my mouth, sounding like my own but yet so different. Her hands grip the steering wheel. My hands. She flips the visor down and looks at me, showing me all the things she's done. Opening valves on Rusty's propane tank. Standing in the window watching Gerald brush his teeth with poisoned toothpaste. She puckers up, smiling at me the way she did in the photos she took with Luke. "That was payback for Conner sleeping with Abbie. He owes us more respect than that, don't you think?"

She flips the visor up and drives away from the police station. "Go back!" I scream at her. She laughs. "I knew you wouldn't like being nosy, but Conner wants you to relive all of our memories, Sierra. And boy do I have some good ones for you."

She heads for the city limits, passing the welcome sign and showing it to me in the rearview. I don't need to ask about my mom. Bobbi is letting me see her too, hanging from a railing in the stairwell leading to the hotel's dank basement. In the room, on the table where I'd set Mom's DVD player up for her, is a note. It's written on hospital letterhead and scrawled in Mom's own handwriting. This one isn't a forgery, though. Bobbi poured liquor down Mom's throat before forcing her to write her own suicide note.

"Thanks for coming back to Poca, Sierra," Bobbi purrs. "It was fun breaking your mommy's spirit. She clawed and fought the way she used to when you were young, but those scars on our arms only made breaking her all the sweeter." She cackles as I fracture further, giving up, my consciousness fading into the dark abyss of nothingness.

"Not so fast, sweet little Sierra, Conner's good girl that he loves enough to go to prison for," she taunts. "I have one more thing to show you." I fight the memory but she won't let me go. I see teenage

Conner underneath me, and the animal she is ravaging him. "Who am I tonight?" she asks him. He flips her over, heated eyes staring right into hers. "Bobbi."

Acknowledgements

"The fear that all this will end. The fear that it won't." ~ Rae Armantrout

Wow! *Sierra* is one of those books that wrote itself backwards in my mind. I saw the end before the beginning and had no idea where the middle would go. Once I began to write, I was surprised, a little repulsed, and positively thrilled! Thank you for taking the journey with me. I couldn't continue without the support of readers and my heart is full because of you. I hope you enjoyed this story as much as I did! Will there be more? Probably. Bobbi is just getting started, and nothing is ever what it seems.

My thanks to Cousin Bobbi for the fun use of her name, and to one of her favorite bands for their inspirational lyrics. I may have bastardized the lines of Iron Maiden's *Fear of the Dark*, but I hope Bobbi and all of their fans enjoy the easter eggs dripped throughout the book.

Nothing I write would ever see the light of day without the patient editing of Anita. Proof Positive is a gem I can't live without. Every mistake in the book is mine because sometimes I can't decide if I'm bawling or balling, and I'm too embarrassed to ask Anita!

This cover is beautiful because of the talented Marianne at Pre-Made Ebook Cover Shop. She never ceases to amaze me.

I'm forever grateful to my husband, son, daughter-in-law, grandpups, grand-demon-kitty, and my fabulous Sadie Jo. They make my life beautiful.

Visit **LeeDawnaBooks.com** to see what's coming next, and to join my newsletter for special announcements!

Also By Lee Dawna

<u>Beller Ties – A four-book stand-alone romantic suspense collection.</u>

Something So Beautiful

Now And Always

Dawn Of Devotion

Marked By Forever

<u>Hinton Thriller Series – A serial-killer thriller trilogy.</u>

Descend

Smother

Rise

Coming **October 31, 2023** – Book 1 of a *Fantasy* Thriller Trilogy. Visit **LeeDawnaBooks.com** to join my mailing list for early release news!

About the Author

Lee Dawna is a thriller and suspense author, and host of the Immortal Monsters Podcast. An avid traveler and outdoorswoman, you may bump into her along a remote trail where a meandering stream whispers her next story.

Visit **LeeDawnaBooks.com** for more on what the author is up to lately, and to **join her mailing list** for special announcements.

Find her on **YouTube** @ImmortalMonsters and @LeeDawnaBooks, and at **Patreon.com/leedawna**